RETURN TO NEW YORK

What Happens in... book three
Part of the *What Happens in Hollywood Universe*

KRISTINA ADAMS

Copyright © 2024 Kristina Adams

All rights reserved.

This book or any part of it must not be reproduced or used in anyway without written permission of the publisher, except for brief quotations used in a book review.

First published in 2018. This edition published in 2024.

Cover image by Elenglush from Adobe Stock. Cover design by Kristina Adams.

To everyone who fights the monsters in their heads everyday. Keep fighting. It's worth it.

SEPTEMBER

ONE

Late. How was she late? She was never late!

Her mum had taught her to always be on time, and if she couldn't be on time, to be early. But her mum wasn't around anymore. She'd never teach her anything ever again. But if it wasn't for her mum and sister's deaths, she wouldn't be about to walk into her first ever photography class.

Fayth stopped outside the door and wiped a tear from the corner of her eye. She was already late – what difference would a couple more minutes make?

If it wasn't for her mum, she wouldn't have met Liam. She may never have left her ex-husband. Her dad may never have sold the family pub.

Oh, for fuck's sake.

She scrubbed at her eyes as they filled with more tears. She could stand there all day playing the What If game, but what difference did it make?

Her mum and sister were dead. She was not. If there were such a thing as ghosts, and her mum and sister found out she was sobbing over them while about to go to her first ever photography class in New York, they'd haunt her arse until she went mad.

She straightened up, lifted her head high, and walked into the room. 'Sorry,' she said as she walked in. Eight people turned to face her. Some looked disapproving, others pitying. They were probably cursing her for being the foreigner that hadn't anticipated rush hour traffic. Except she had. She'd just forgot to set an alarm.

'Don't worry about it, we were just about to start the introductions,' said the man at the front of a circle of chairs. He perched his glasses on top of his head and gestured to an empty chair beside him. 'Take a seat.'

'Thanks.' Fayth sat down between him and a woman with long, wavy brown hair. She wore a yellow flower garland and a matching yellow dress. It made her look like she belonged in the 1970s.

'I hate ice breakers, so we're just going to say our names. It's up to you if you say anything else,' said the man that had welcomed her. 'I'm Jasper, your course leader. I've been teaching photography now for about five years, and I've been a photographer for over twenty.' He patted the top of his head. 'And I've been bald for longer than I care to remember.'

The class chuckled.

Jasper looked to the person on his left. He wore a newspaper boy hat and a tweed jacket. It was mid-twenties outside, and the air con in the room barely seemed to do anything. Even Fayth's permanently cold best friend Hollie would've roasted in those temperatures. How was he not on fire? 'Rupert,' he said. There was an awkward pause. Everyone waited, expecting him to say something else, but he didn't.

Finally, the old woman to his left spoke: 'I'm Liesel,' she said. 'I'm a retired nurse.'

'Arthur,' said the old man beside her. 'My day job's looking after this one.' He nudged Liesel. She glared at him. The rest of the room laughed.

Would she and Liam be that cute one day?

Next to Arthur was Marisol. She tossed her long, dark hair, revealing hoop earrings that almost touched her shoulders. 'I work with a lot of charities for events, but I'm sick of paying for shitty photographers. So that's why I'm here!'

'I'm Gale,' said a man with a thick, ginger beard that

reminded Fayth of her ex-husband, Patrick. A few weeks ago she would've suppressed a shudder at the thought. But after someone had almost killed her, he'd come to see her and they'd reached an understanding.

But their stalker…

Focus. Stay in the moment. She had to focus.

She squeezed her eyes shut and focused on the next person that spoke.

'I'm Akia,' said a guy a couple of seats away from her. He recoiled into himself, as if getting attention was the worst thing in the world. Then again, Fayth was inclined to agree a lot of the time.

'I'm Maisie,' said the girl on her right brightly. 'I'm a freelance business analyst.'

Fayth hadn't seen that one coming. She'd expected her to say she worked for Amnesty International or something. Then again, if being friends with celebrities had taught her anything, it was that you really couldn't judge someone based on how they looked.

Everyone turned to Fayth. 'I'm Fayth,' she said with a smile. 'As you can probably tell, I'm from Scotland. Feel free to say something if you don't know what I'm on about. I can't understand myself half the time either.'

Everyone in the class – except for Rupert – laughed. What was his problem?

Jasper stood up and put his hands together. 'Now that we're all acquainted, let's get right to it. The focus this morning will be on theory, then we'll break for lunch and take some photos this afternoon. Most of our classes will follow a similar pattern. The end of our time together will culminate in a showcase at a local gallery run by one of my former students. We'll each pick our favourite photos to display, then sell them off to attendees.'

Sell them? Fayth had known the course would end with a show, but she hadn't realised attendees would be able to buy their photos. That was weird, wasn't it? Something she'd spent time creating hanging on someone else's wall. But then, how else were professional photographers supposed to make their money? And she *did* want to be a professional photographer. Didn't she?

Jasper pressed a button, and a PowerPoint appeared on a screen behind him. There were several different shots: some landscapes, some portraits, some close-ups, some wide shots. 'What do you think makes a good photograph?'

Subject.

An awkward pause filled the air.

Lighting.

No one spoke.

Exposure.

Silence.

Angle.

It was like being back in school.

Aperture.

Oh for the love of—

'Lighting.'

Had she really just said that? She'd always been told off at school for not 'participating' enough. Being an introvert wasn't allowed at school. Not speaking up in class meant you didn't know what was going on and weren't paying attention.

'Thank you,' said Jasper. 'Anything else?'

The room fell silent again. Fayth rolled her eyes.

'Angle,' said Maisie. She shifted. Fayth caught sight of her shoes. Doc Martins. With a floral dress. Fayth approved.

'Thank you, Maisie.' He walked over to the whiteboard to the left of the screen, took a pen from his pocket, and started writing on the whiteboard. 'Lighting and angle. Anything else?'

'Exposure,' said Rupert.

'Yes!' said Jasper, writing that on the whiteboard too. 'What else?'

The room fell silent again.

Subject.
Nobody.
Really? No one?
'Subject,' Fayth said aloud.

'Yes! What you're taking a photograph of is crucial!' He scribbled it on to the whiteboard. 'Where you put the focus also makes a huge difference. For example—' He switched slides to a photo of a bee hovering over a flower. 'Take this photo. What's wrong with it?'

'It's confused,' said Maisie.

The class laughed. They were finding the same things funny. That was a good sign, right?

'Why?' asked Jasper.

'There's too much going on. Everything is in focus. The bee is pretty, but the background is so busy you don't know where to focus your eyes,' said Maisie.

'Yes, exactly,' said Jasper. 'Anything else?'

'The angle is off,' said Gale. 'The bee is perfectly centred, which is actually a bad thing for photos. You're better off using something like the golden ratio or the rule of thirds.'

'Yes! The positioning of the subject in your photo is also vital.' He added that to the list on the whiteboard. 'If you're not sure what the golden ratio or rule of thirds is, don't worry as we'll cover those later on.' He pressed a remote, and another photo appeared on screen. 'What about this one?'

'The photographer has zoomed in on the bee and put the background in a soft focus, guiding your eyes towards the bee,' said Fayth.

'It's a better angle, too,' added Gale. 'You get a bee's-eye-view of the world.'

'Yes!' Jasper cried, a little over-enthusiastically. 'It's even more crucial with people. I'm going to need a volunteer. Any takers?'

Everyone seemed to shrink into their seats.

'Maisie? That flower garland would look great on camera,' said Jasper with a cheeky grin.

'Oh go on then,' said Maisie, flashing Fayth a mischievous smile as she stood up.

'Are the flowers real?' he asked as the class made their way to the back of the room where four backdrops and lighting kits were set up. They circled around one of them.

Maisie touched her flower garland. 'No.'

'I'm disappointed. I expect you to come in with a real one next week.'

'Sure. I'll make one for you, too.'

The class chuckled.

'And that, folks, is lesson number one,' said Jasper. 'Establish a rapport with your subject. The more comfortable they are around you, the better the shot you'll take. If your subject feels awkward, it will come across on camera.'

With all the rushing around, Fayth had forgot to pack a notebook or her laptop. She grabbed her phone from her pocket and typed some notes about establishing a rapport with her subjects. All the photos she'd taken in the past had either been of family and friends, pets, or landscapes. It was easy to make them feel at ease. But if she wanted to make a living as a photographer, she'd have to find a way to establish a rapport with strangers, too. But then, hadn't she already spent years doing that as a bartender? Just because her dad had sold the Cock and Bull, that didn't mean that she'd forgotten how to talk to people…

'Maisie, if you could stand on that X right there for me please,' said Jasper, pointing to an X that had been marked out in duct tape on the floor. Maisie did as instructed. 'Now, just stand facing me, your arms by your side, looking straight ahead.' Maisie narrowed her eyes. 'You'll see why in a minute,' he added.

The pose he'd chosen was completely unflattering. Was that the point? To show how a pose can make all the difference? Jasper took a few photos, then got Maisie to turn to the side with one foot in front of the other, her hands on her hips, and her head turned to the camera. A typical Hollywood pose. He pressed a few buttons on his camera, and the two images appeared on the screen at the front of the room. They returned to their seats. 'You see the difference a change of pose makes? The reason everyone says the camera adds ten pounds is because, if it gets you at the wrong angle, it does. A photo is a snapshot – you only get to see the full picture if the photographer knows what they're doing.'

*

'Cool shoes,' said Fayth as she and Maisie waited for the lift at lunchtime.

Maisie pulled up her dress a little to show off her Doc Martens. 'Thanks,' said Maisie. 'I've had them forever. I love your shirt.'

Fayth beamed. Her usual outfit was jeans and a t-shirt, but to make her feel empowered she'd worn one of her Hollie Baxter exclusives – an umbrella-patterned blouse and black chinos. Having a fashion designer for a best friend had its perks. 'Thanks. It's from my friend's fashion line.'

'Your friend is a fashion designer? That's so cool!'

'Yeah,' said Fayth with a proud smile. The lift arrived, and the two of them climbed into it.

'Say, want to grab some lunch? I know this really cool sandwich place around the corner.'

'Sure, sounds good,' said Fayth.

*

Fayth and Maisie spent their lunchtime eating fancy sandwiches and talking about nothing in particular. When they returned to class, Jasper got each of them to pick a piece of paper out of a hat. 'If you're an odd number,' said Jasper, 'I want you to go stand at one of the setups at the back of the room.'

Rupert, Akia, Liesel, and Maisie stood up and walked to where the lighting kits were set up.

'OK now what numbers do the rest of you have?' Jasper turned to Fayth.

'Eight.'

'Fayth, you're with Rupert on the end.' He pointed to the setup to the right.

There was something about Rupert that made her uncomfortable, but she couldn't work out what. Every time she'd tried to speak to him, he'd ignored her. In group discussions he'd even cut her off when she spoke. Fayth knew she couldn't always work with people she liked, though, so she decided to try to make the most of it. Even if that did mean talking through gritted teeth.

'So whereabouts in New York are you from?' Fayth asked as she attached her camera to the tripod.

'Huh?' said Rupert, looking up from his phone.

'Whereabouts in New York are you from?' she repeated.

'Queens,' he said.

'I've never been there,' she said. 'What's it like?'

'I'm sure it's not your kind of place.'

What was *that* supposed to mean? She decided to let it go and focus on the task at hand. 'If you stand on the cross and turn slightly.' Rupert did as instructed. 'That's it. Now fold your arms and look over my right shoulder.' He did that, too. 'Hold that!' Fayth switched on her camera and began to snap. Something didn't look right. 'Lift your head an inch or so.' He lifted it several. 'Not that far. try to keep your chin parallel to the floor.' Fayth adjusted one of the lights so that it was directly in his face.

'Are you *trying* to blind me?' he snapped.

'Sorry,' said Fayth, angling it away.

No matter how hard he made it for her, she was going to

take a decent photo of him.

After an hour of experimentation, they returned to the circle and analysed the photos. Jasper praised Fayth's photos for Rupert's power pose, but Marisol made fun of his expression, saying that he looked constipated. Fayth had had to force herself not to laugh. He'd definitely seemed emotionally constipated, that was for sure. She hoped that they'd have to work with someone else when they swapped, but she had no such luck. It was Rupert's turn to take her photo.

And he was terrible at it.

He offered her no direction. She knew what looked good on camera, but she was no model. She didn't know her angles, and without access to a screen, how was she supposed to work them out? A good photographer offered you direction. Rupert barely even spoke. He couldn't have looked more bored. He'd never make it as a photographer if he couldn't direct his subjects.

Jasper stood over Rupert's shoulder, watching for a minute. He approached Rupert, smiling. 'Have you thought about changing the angle? You could get closer and go for a low-angled close up, or go further back and get her whole outfit in.' He looked up at Fayth. 'Which is great, by the way.'

She really needed to wear Hollie's clothes more often. Every time she wore them, she got compliments. If only she was as coordinated as her best friend. Without Hollie's guidance, she always got into a panic about what to wear with what, even when Hollie insisted she'd sent her stuff to help her form a capsule wardrobe. Whatever one of those was.

'I wanted to take a midshot, but she isn't taking my direction,' said Rupert.

Fayth's back stiffened. He hadn't *given* her any direction. She pursed her lips, but didn't say anything.

Jasper shot Fayth an apologetic look. 'Make it clear to

her what your vision is for the photo. The clearer you make your vision to the subject, the easier it will be for them to bring it to life.'

They stood awkwardly for a few moments. Rupert kept his hand on his camera but didn't take any photos. Once Jasper had walked off to help Marisol, he resumed taking photos exactly as he had a few minutes before. Sigh.

As expected, the photos of Fayth were terrible. She returned to Liam's apartment a few hours later feeling disheartened. The poor photos weren't her fault, but she was still embarrassed. She'd looked frumpy, grumpy, and had somehow gained a second chin. While a great photograph said just as much about the photographer as it did the subject, she desperately hoped nobody would ever see those photos. Every time she'd tried to change her pose or pull a different expression, Rupert had shown disapproval and made her go back to the terrible position he wanted her in. If that was his attitude to everything he did, she was surprised he'd made it into his thirties.

'Hey, how was photography class?' asked Liam as she walked into the games room. He sat at a desk in the corner, playing *World of Warcraft*. He took off his headset and signed out, spinning his chair to face her.

She leaned against the pool table. 'It was…interesting. There's a lot to think about.' She didn't want to go into Rupert. Despite his dislike of her plaguing her thoughts, she'd got on fine with everyone else.

'Did you make any friends?'

'I did actually,' she said, smiling. 'Her name's Maisie. She doesn't own a TV.'

Liam scoffed. 'Sure she doesn't.'

'No she really doesn't. She has no idea about pop culture.'

'You really do attract the weird ones,' said Liam, standing up and kissing her forehead.

She squirmed. 'You know you're insulting yourself,

right?'

'Mmm. I work in Hollywood. Being weird is a prerequisite. Speaking of which,' said Liam, leaning beside her. He ran his hand through his hair. Oh no. What horrible Hollywood thing had happened now? 'Trinity messaged me earlier. She wants to meet with you.'

He said it so fast she almost thought she'd misheard him, but the words 'Trinity' and 'meet' had come across loud and clear. What could that sociopath possibly want with her? Wasn't it enough that she'd caused most of the public to hate Fayth for 'stealing' Liam from her and caused one of her crazed fans to try to kill Fayth and Liam? What more could she possibly want? A kidney?

Fayth turned her head to Liam, her jaw tight. 'Why?'

He shrugged.

'What's her underlying motive?'

He shrugged again.

'What *do* you know?'

'That she wants to meet with you.' He hadn't met her gaze since the topic of Trinity had come up. She hadn't even known they were still in contact. He changed his phone number all the time to stop the press from getting hold of him. How'd his sociopathic ex-girlfriend get hold of it? More importantly, *why* did she have it? If Trinity wanted to speak to her that badly, couldn't she have contacted Fayth herself?

Reasons why Trinity would want to meet ran through Fayth's mind faster than items on *The Generation Game* conveyor belt. She'd written a song about Fayth and wanted to make sure Fayth was OK with it. Ha. Like Trinity would ask for permission to do something like that. She wanted Fayth to take her photo for her new album. No, she probably had photographer frenemies way better equipped for something like that. She had a rare blood type and there was a chance that Fayth was a match. No, even when desperate Trinity wouldn't ask her for help. What did she really want?

'There has to be a reason. There's always an underlying motive with her,' said Fayth.

'I know,' agreed Liam, 'But I don't know what it is.'

'So, what? She just texts you out of nowhere and asks if we can catch up over a coffee? Doesn't that seem weird to you?'

'I never said it wasn't weird, just that I don't know any more than that. Tea?'

Of course he'd change the subject.

*

Fayth did need tea. It had been a long day, and she was exhausted. She went into the kitchen and reached to get two mugs from the cupboard…but the cupboard was empty. A pile of used mugs sat in the kitchen sink. How had he used them all while she'd been out? She'd washed up before she'd left that morning! *And* his cleaner had been in!

She tipped the water out of the mugs in the sink and slammed them onto the side.

'What's up with you?' said Liam as she filled the sink with water.

'How have you used every single mug while I've been out? Your cleaner only left a couple of hours ago!'

'Different drink, different mug,' said Liam, nonchalant.

She shook her head, fishing the washing up liquid out from under the sink and slamming it onto the countertop. The damn stuff was staying out to remind him not to leave things out and let them fester.

'It's fine, we'll just wash up what we need and the cleaner can do the rest in the morning.'

Fayth tensed. She turned the tap off, then spun to face him. 'Are you serious? Do you even hear yourself right now?'

'They're just mugs, Fayth.'

'They're covered in all sorts of bacteria! The longer you leave them dirty, the harder it is to get the stains out. Doesn't that bother you?'

He shrugged. 'I can always replace them.'

Fayth took a deep breath and frantically scrubbed at a *Tomb Raider* mug with tea stains on.

'What's really up?' said Liam. 'You're not seriously pissed about a few mugs, are you?'

Was she?

'Yes. No. Maybe.' She slammed the mug onto the draining board and turned back to him. 'Yes, it bothers me that you expect other people to do everything for you. No, that's not the only thing that's bothering me.'

Liam perched on a stool by the counter.

'I didn't realise Trinity had your new number,' said Fayth, avoiding eye contact.

'What do you think I'm going to do? Go running back to her? Come on, Fayth.'

'You know what? Forget it.' Fayth dried her hands and went into the living room, closing the door in the hopes that he'd take the hint. Her laptop was still on the antique coffee table where she'd left it the night before. She picked it up and opened it, hoping that Hollie was online. She was. Of course she was. She was *always* online.

Hollie called her before Fayth even had a chance to message her. 'Hey,' said Hollie. A room full of fabric and clothing was visible in the background.

'Hey,' said Fayth, settling onto the sofa.

'What's up? You look like you want to smash something,' said Hollie.

Fayth filled her in. Hollie listened while sewing something by hand. When Fayth had finished, Hollie nodded, concentrating on her stitches. 'Just a second, almost finished.' She finished stitching, placed the garment on the bed behind her, then turned back to Fayth.

'You know, it'd be quite nice to have a cleaner,' said

Hollie.

'That's because your room always looks like a bomb went off in it.'

Hollie turned to the mess behind her, then back to Fayth. She shrugged. 'I think you're getting worked up over nothing. You and Liam are from different worlds. You're bound to have different ways of working. You just need to find ways to compromise.'

Fayth sighed. 'I suppose.'

'And as for Trinity…what do you want to do about it?'

She'd been so busy wondering what Trinity's underlying motives were that she hadn't even thought about whether or not to actually meet with her. 'I guess I'm curious,' said Fayth, 'but am I curious enough to meet up with her?'

'Only you know that. But you don't have to answer right away. You're in New York for the next few months. Why not wait and see what happens?'

'I guess I could. It's not like she could hate me any more than she already does.'

'Can't argue with that,' said Hollie.

There was a knock at the living room door.

'He knocks in his own apartment? That's cute,' said Hollie, 'you should keep him.'

Fayth rolled her eyes, closed her laptop, and opened the door. Liam stood before her, his head bowed and his hands stuffed into his pockets. 'She got my number from my agent. He still thinks we should work together. She told him that's what she wanted to talk about when she asked him for my number.'

'Manipulative as ever,' mumbled Fayth.

Liam wrapped his arms around her. 'I don't want anything to do with her either, but I can't avoid her. You get that, right?'

Fayth nodded, hugging him back. 'I'm sorry.'

'Me too,' he said, kissing the top of her head.

'It's up to you if you meet her or not. Nobody seems to

know what she wants.'

'You asked?' Fayth lifted her head.

'I asked a few people I can trust. Trinity doesn't give much away unless it helps her to get what she wants, though.'

Two

'So tell me more about photography class,' Liam asked as they sat in a Japanese restaurant an hour later. 'I thought you'd be buzzing when you got home but you weren't.'

Fayth ran her hand over her face. She'd put on some make-up, *just in case*. They were at a posh restaurant, and she had on another of Hollie's designs. Oh, and she was with one of the world's biggest film stars. Given the press's penchant for photographing her at unflattering angles, she thought a little bit of make-up couldn't hurt.

'Campbell?'

She sighed. If only she was a better liar. 'The class was great, but there was this one guy who just didn't seem to like me.' She sipped her water. They really needed to hurry up with the wine.

'What do you mean?' he asked, flicking his head so that his dark, floppy hair was out of his eyes.

'We had to take each other's photos, and he barked orders at me like I was a stupid child. When it was my turn to take his photo, he refused to take any instruction from me. He was fine with everyone else, though.'

'You can't get on with everyone, I guess,' he said, squeezing her knee.

'I suppose. How was your day?'

'Funny you should ask,' he said, a cheesy grin appearing on his face. 'I got offered a role.'

'That's great!' said Fayth. She leaned over and kissed him. 'In what?'

'It doesn't have a title yet, but it's directed by Baz Luhrmann and starts filming in January. I'd only be on set for a few days as it isn't a major role, but Baz Luhrmann!'

'That's amazing!' she said, reaching over the table and squeezing his hand. 'Two roles in three months. Get you!'

He gave a small laugh.

'When do you leave for LA again?' she asked.

'End of October. I'll only be gone a week. You'll be too busy with your new photographer friends by then to even notice I'm gone.'

'Course I won't. I've got used to having you around.'

It wasn't just that – when Liam went off to LA, it would be the first time she'd been on her own since someone had almost killed them. They'd been the only ones still awake at the pub (Liam's bodyguard, Wade, was passed out on the sofa), when the electricity had cut out. Little did they realise it was Liam's stalker that had switched it off and she was downstairs waiting for them. If it hadn't been for Fayth and Liam's teamwork and quick thinking, his stalker might've done much more serious damage to them both.

'Aren't you cute?' said Liam.

It bugged Fayth that Liam seemed fine about it all when she wasn't. She hadn't brought it up with him, though. It wasn't his fault he dealt with trauma better than she did. She just needed some time to recover, that was all. He hadn't been physically hurt by the whole thing – she'd been hit in the back of the head with the gun. Whenever she thought about the heavy metal object colliding with her skull, the back of her head twinged. She was lucky it had only given her a mild concussion. Hadn't it?

Three

Fayth decided against meeting up with Trinity. That woman had done enough damage already. Agreeing to meet with her was an olive branch that she didn't deserve. Whatever Trinity's motives were, she'd never know. And that was just fine so long as Trinity stayed as far away from her as possible.

Besides, Fayth had more important things to think about: Liam's birthday was a few weeks away, and she still hadn't got him anything. How could she? The guy had everything he wanted. Anything he didn't want he could buy. What was she supposed to buy someone like that?

After spending an hour browsing the internet and coming up with a fat lot of nothing, Fayth Skyped Hollie. She was unpicking something.

'What can I get Liam for his birthday?' asked Fayth. She got up and started pacing the living room. She'd acquired it as her space, since Liam spent most of his time in the games room on *World of Warcraft*.

Hollie looked up from the garment she was unpicking. 'You know I suck with presents, right?'

'No you don't.'

'I do if it's not something I've made.' Hollie stopped unpicking and glared at Fayth. 'You know, it's really distracting trying to unpick and talk to someone who keeps disappearing on and offscreen.'

'Sorry,' said Fayth, sitting down.

Hollie scratched her head with the unpicker. 'If he *has*

everything, don't give him anything. *Do* something instead.'

'Like what?'

'I don't know! You're his girlfriend, not me.'

'We've only been going out a few months! That's not long enough to figure out what to buy someone! I still struggle to come up with ideas for Dad and Brooke!'

'Why don't you ask Tate, then? She's known him forever.'

'She's in Jamaica,' said Fayth. Tate was one of Liam's oldest friends and always happy to help people, but Fayth wasn't going to interrupt her holiday for something as silly as a birthday present.

'So? She loves helping people. She wouldn't mind the distraction.'

'She'd try to turn it into a circus,' said Fayth.

Hollie tilted her head. 'Possibly. Why don't you write some ideas down and see if you like any of them?'

'I don't have time for that! He could be back from the gym any minute!'

'So you don't have time to write down a few ideas? Come on. It doesn't take *that* long,' said Hollie.

Fayth sighed. 'Thanks for not helping.'

'Any time,' said Hollie. She turned her attention back to her unpicking and hung up. Some help she'd been. She could speak to one of Liam's staff, but that would be weird. How well did they *really* know him? Sure, they were his friends, but were they the kinds of friends to get him presents? Would they tell him if she asked them about it? Their loyalty was to him, not her, after all.

There was one other person she could ask. But should she? They hadn't exactly left things in a good place. She didn't even know where he was or if he'd even respond. She'd heard rumours that he'd gone home to Texas, but she wasn't sure if they were true. Things got awkward between Fayth and Liam whenever the topic of Hollie's ex came up, so they tried to avoid mentioning him. Liam was still close to him, but Fayth was still Hollie's best friend. She couldn't betray Hollie, could she?

But then, was it betrayal? Hollie couldn't stop her from talking to someone. It was up to Fayth whom she spoke to.

Desperate times…

She reached for the button to send him a message, but hit call instead. She couldn't hit the cancel button fast enough. He answered immediately. Wow. She hadn't expected that.

His hair was longer and swept back from his face, and he'd finally shaved off his terrible beard. He really had looked awful with a beard. The swept-back look suited him. His blue eyes were narrowed, his mouth quirked into a small smile. There was a darkness to his expression that he hadn't shaken since the last time they'd seen each other. Was there anything she could do to help him? No. It wasn't her place to counsel Astin. He had other people who were better suited to that.

'Hi,' squeaked Fayth.

'Hey,' said Astin in his Texan drawl.

'Hi,' said Fayth again, shifting in her seat and looking away from the camera. Was it OK to be talking to her best friend's ex after everything he'd done? Was it? 'How are you?'

She didn't have to say anything to Hollie. What Hollie didn't know wouldn't hurt her.

'You know,' said Astin with a shrug. Given he'd had major surgery on his upper spine six months earlier, the fact that he could manage a shrug was a huge deal. 'How's New York?'

'Who told you I was in New York?'

'Liam. He really likes having you around.'

Fayth smiled. 'Really?'

'Yeah,' said Astin, his smile growing. It was a hollow smile, though. As if he was doing it because he felt that he should, not because he actually felt anything.

'Listen, I know it's unfair of me to ask and you can say

no, but—'

'You need birthday present ideas,' interjected Astin.

'How'd you know?'

'There's less than a month until his birthday. You'd only call me if you were desperate.'

'Sorry,' said Fayth, looking away from the camera.

'Have you got any starting points?'

'Well Hol—' She cut herself off. Would it bother him if she mentioned Hollie? Hollie still couldn't hear his name without looking like someone had jabbed a needle into her arm. 'Someone else suggested I should do something with him.'

'"*Do* something"?' echoed Astin, a teasing note in his voice.

'Not like that! Well maybe. I mean—ugh, you know what I mean. The guy can literally buy or do whatever he wants. He has an endless stream of money. What can I possibly give someone like that?'

'Well maybe Ho—' He flinched. That answered that question. 'Maybe she's on to something. What connects you? It doesn't have to be anything crazy. Sometimes it's the simple things that have the biggest impact.'

OCTOBER

ONE

As September turned into October, the stifling New York heat finally became closer to a temperature Fayth was used to. Unfortunately, Fayth wasn't prepared for the dramatic change in temperature. Fortunately, Hollie sent her some more clothes (which Fayth insisted on sending her the money for) to keep her warm. She headed to her first photography class of October in jeans and a jumper, and a green trench coat Hollie had sent her.

'Your coat is so cute!' cooed Maisie as she walked in.

Fayth caught sight of Rupert glaring out of the corner of her eye. She ignored him. 'Thanks. It's one of Hollie's.'

'I like it,' said Maisie, admiring it as Fayth took it off.

Thankfully, Fayth was paired with Maisie that week. Rupert was with Liesel. Surprisingly, he didn't lose his temper with her. He was calm and patient – the exact opposite of how he was with Fayth whenever they worked together. What had she done to piss him off so much?

They reconvened after their photoshoots to discuss their finished photographs. Almost everyone in the class had improved – even Liesel, who admitted to being partially sighted. The only person who hadn't improved was Rupert. The lighting in his shots of Liesel was unflattering; she had shadows under her chin and under her eyes, making her look tired and even older than her eighty-something years. Had he paid any attention to what Jasper had said the last few weeks? Surely he must've learned something? Why bother paying for classes if he wasn't willing to listen to what the teacher had to say?

After class, Fayth and Maisie went for a coffee. Or, in Fayth's case, tea. Maisie was always happy and smiley, which helped to balance out the bad vibes Fayth got from Rupert. Her not owning a TV also meant that she wouldn't go all giddy when she met Liam. When Fayth mentioned Liam's *Highwater* film franchise, Maisie had no idea what she was talking about. Fayth took that as a good sign and invited Liam to join them. He hadn't been out much recently except to go to the gym and the occasional audition. Most of his friends were away, so she figured getting out and socialising would be good for him.

But as they sat waiting for him in the coffee shop, she began to regret her decision. There were lots of people about and it was Wade's day off. What if some crazy person descended on them? Guns were legal there. Nobody would care if they saw someone with a handgun. Or worse...

Fayth twitched her foot under the table as Maisie explained her logic for not owning a TV. 'It's all so formulaic these days. It bores me.'

'I know what you mean,' said Fayth.

'I prefer to read a book.'

'What are you reading at the minute?'

'*The Beautiful and Damned*.'

'Impressive.'

'No. Having read *War and Peace* is impressive.'

'Have you read that?'

Maisie snorted. 'God, no. I have better things to do with my time.'

'I tend to read more modern stuff myself,' admitted Fayth. 'The classics remind me too much of school.'

'I get that.' Maisie sipped her black coffee. 'Say, what's the deal with you and Rupert? He seems fine until you walk in, then it's like someone shoves a stick up his ass.'

'You've noticed, then.'

Maisie nodded. 'It's hard not to. Do you two know each

other or something?'

'I met him the same day I met you. I don't get what I've done to piss him off so much.'

'Maybe he's got a thing for you,' said Maisie.

Fayth snorted. 'Yeah. Right.'

'He's widowed. You never know.'

'What's that got to do with anything?'

'Maybe he's looking for a rebound. You've got that exotic foreigner thing going for you,' said Maisie, waving her arms as she spoke.

'I'm Scottish. That's hardly exotic.'

'I dunno. I can't understand what you're saying half the time.'

Fayth stuck her tongue out at Maisie.

The door to the coffee shop opened, and Liam walked in. It was time to find out just how much Maisie really knew about pop culture. He approached them, a broad smile on his face. He was in *Liam York, actor* mode. Just in case. 'Hey.' He put his arm around Fayth's waist and kissed her cheek.

'Hey,' said Fayth.

'Sup. I'm Maisie.'

'Liam.' He sat on the chair beside Fayth and sipped her tea. Cheeky bugger. As if he couldn't afford his own.

If Maisie recognised Liam, she didn't show it. There was no acknowledgement on her face whatsoever. She gave him the same friendly smile she did everyone else. 'How long have you two been dating?'

'Er…' Liam looked to Fayth for confirmation.

Fayth rolled her eyes.

Maisie giggled.

'Three months.'

'Really? You've got that old married couple vibe going on,' said Maisie.

'Do we?' said Fayth, unable to hide her smile. She liked having the old married couple vibe with Liam. She hoped they *would* be an old married couple one day. Well, without the marriage part. She'd done that already.

Maisie nodded. She pointed to Fayth's cup of tea, which Liam still held on to.

Fayth shook her head. 'You'd think he's broke.'

'I am,' said Liam.

'Yeah. Sure you are,' said Fayth.

'Hey, I'll have you know I'm unemployed right now,' said Liam.

'Only for a few more weeks. And besides, unemployed and broke aren't the same. I was employed and broke,' said Fayth.

'What do you do?' Maisie asked Liam.

Fayth and Liam exchanged glances. To tell her the truth, or not to tell her the truth?

'What? He's not a stripper or something, is he?' said Maisie, her gaze flitting between them.

Liam laughed. 'Why? You think I'm hot enough to be?'

'Don't answer that,' said Fayth. 'His ego is big enough already.'

Liam shrugged. 'Comes with the territory.'

Maisie knitted her eyebrows. She was clearly clueless.

Fayth liked her too much to lie to her. 'Remember the *Highwater* films I was on about?'

'Yeah,' said Maisie.

She looked at Liam.

'What? He worked on them?'

Liam laughed.

'You really don't watch TV, do you?' said Fayth.

Maisie shook her head. Her plaited hair tickled her neck as she did so.

Fayth opened the browser on her phone and searched for a *Highwater* poster. She picked one with Liam stood in the centre, staring right at the camera. He had on his character's signature green combat shorts and ripped black t-shirt. And a gun in his hand. Fayth had forgot about the gun. She quickly turned her phone to Maisie and showed her the photo. Fayth didn't need any more reminders about guns.

Maisie's mouth fell open. Her eyes flitted from the photo to Liam and back again a few times. 'I really do live under a rock, don't I?'

Fayth and Liam nodded.

Maisie shrugged. 'Big film star or no, as far as I'm concerned, you're just Fayth's boyfriend.'

Liam grinned. 'I'm happy to be known as that.'

'And since you're technically unemployed right now, really, that's all you are,' said Fayth with a playful smirk.

'I'll have you know I have *two* jobs coming up!' He turned to Maisie. 'See what I have to put up with?'

'I think she's funny,' said Maisie.

'You haven't lived with her,' said Liam.

'You've been together two months and you live together already?'

'We lived together first. Kind of,' said Fayth. 'Liam likes to run away from his problems, so he came to see me in Scotland.'

'You were ill! I wanted to make sure you were all right!' And he thought hiding out in New York would protect him from his stalker, but Fayth was glad he didn't mention that part.

'I wasn't *that* ill,' said Fayth.

'So I used it as an excuse to spend more time with you. Sue me.'

'You guys are killing me with cuteness right now!' squealed Maisie.

'Sorry,' said Fayth, shrinking into her seat.

'No, no, continue. I love it! It's like watching a chick flick unravel right in front of me.'

'Maybe that could be your next role: leading man in a chick flick,' suggested Fayth.

Liam stared at her, deadpan. 'Do you have any idea how many terrible chick flicks I've turned down?'

'No,' said Fayth.

'Neither do I. I lost count.'

Fayth and Maisie giggled.

Liam lifted the tea to take another sip. He lowered it, staring into the mug.

'Did you finish my cuppa?' said Fayth.

'Uh…' Liam stood up. 'Anyone want another drink?'

Fayth shook her head. 'I'll have another tea, please. Greedy git.'

'I'll have whatever it is you two are fighting over,' said Maisie.

'It's just tea,' said Fayth.

'I think it's about time I tasted what all the fuss is about. If I don't like it, you two can fight over it,' said Maisie.

'Us? Fight?' said Liam. He flashed her his trademark cheeky grin, then headed for the counter.

'So…you're really dating a celebrity?' said Maisie.

Fayth nodded. Was this the part when Maisie went into fangirl mode?

'Cool,' said Maisie. 'I wonder. Could that be why Rupert's weird with you?'

'What do you mean?'

'If he knows about your famous boyfriend, he could be jealous.'

Fayth snorted. 'Don't be silly. I don't have anything to be jealous of.'

*

On the drive home, they got caught in traffic. The police had blocked off the road. Fayth couldn't see why, but she could see police officers walking around with guns. She curled her hands into fists and clenched her jaw. Why did guns have to be everywhere in New York? She hadn't noticed them that much last time, though. Was she more aware of them because of what had happened?

She instinctively put her hand to the back of her head. The lump from being hit with a gun had long healed, but the psychological wounds refused to follow suit.

'You all right?' asked Liam.

'Mm-hmm,' said Fayth through gritted teeth.

Liam narrowed his eyes, but he didn't press it. He wouldn't in front of his driver Thalia, and for that, Fayth was grateful.

Until they got home and were alone, when he asked her again.

'I'm fine. It doesn't matter,' she insisted. She didn't want to worry him. It was her problem – she'd deal with it in her own time.

'You're not, though. You were fine when we left the cafe, but you started acting weird on the way home. What happened?'

'Nothing. I told you. It doesn't matter.'

Liam frowned.

'Fine. I saw the gun and it reminded me of what happened at the pub!'

'Oh,' he said. Was that it? Why didn't it bother him? Why was he so unfazed by everything?

Fayth crossed her arms over her chest. 'How are you so calm? You had a stalker. She pointed a gun to your head! And you act like nothing happened!'

'Your upbringing was a lot more sheltered than mine was. That wasn't the first time I'd seen a gun. Hell, shooting her wasn't the first time I'd fired one.'

Fayth took a step back. 'Wait…what?'

'My dad keeps one at home. Tate goes to the shooting range as stress relief. The people in my life aren't as anti-gun as people in the UK are.'

'That's not the point! She *stalked* you. She found your phone number and email address. She even rang the pub! Doesn't that freak you out?'

'It did at the time, yeah. But now…' He shrugged. So

nonchalant. How? *How?* He walked over to her and put his arm around her waist. 'I have you, and I have Wade, and security cameras and extra security guards just a call away if I want them. Is that what you need? Security?'

'No! That's not it! It's...' What? What did she want? What did she need?

Liam pulled her into a hug. 'Whatever you need, just say it.'

Goddamnit, she was trying to be mad at him. She couldn't be mad at someone so cute. Begrudgingly, she hugged him back, inhaling his familiar scent of cinnamon and sandalwood.

'I don't know,' she confessed. 'I wish I did.'

'Well when you figure it out, I'm right here. Always.' He kissed the top of her head. 'How about we go for some sushi?'

Fayth wrinkled her nose. 'I'm not eating raw fish.'

'See what I mean about sheltered?' he said.

She pulled away from him and crossed her arms. He pulled her back. 'I'm just saying there's no harm in trying new things. You wanted to explore the big, wide world, didn't you? Isn't that why you're happy your dad sold the pub?'

'Well...'

He'd got her there, and he knew it.

Two

Fayth and Liam didn't really have a 'first date'. Not in the traditional sense. He'd still been in a relationship with Trinity the first time they'd hung out. Technically Fayth had still been married too, but she and her ex-husband had been separated for months by then. She and Liam had only hung out because Hollie had wanted to go on a date with Astin, and Liam had agreed to babysit Fayth. If she'd known how things would turn out, would she still have agreed to spending time with him? Sure, she loved Liam now, but if she could've protected Hollie from the pain of breaking up with Astin, and herself from the pain of waking up in hot sweats feeling the gun hit the back of her head…

Fayth shook her head and tried to pull herself back to the present. She had Liam. Something good had come out of all the pain. If she focused on that, the rest didn't seem so bad. Mostly.

They'd spent their first non-date wandering around Central Park. And that's exactly what she planned to recreate for his birthday. She'd booked a pedicab for them to ride in, then planned a stop at a hotdog stand. Except without Liam breaking another paparazzo's camera. Hopefully.

Just like last time, Liam's chauffeur Thalia drove them there, then waited in a nearby car park. She didn't seem to mind waiting – she always had a paperback stashed in the glove compartment. Wade tagged along behind, keeping enough of a distance that he couldn't hear their conversation (or that's what she told herself, anyway), but staying close enough that he could protect them.

'I thought instead of giving you something for your birthday, we could recreate our first pseudo-date,' said Fayth, slipping her hand into Liam's as golden leaves crunched under their feet.

'Have you planned a paparazzo that needs his camera breaking, too?'

Fayth nudged him. 'No. I thought we could skip that part.'

'Spoilsport,' said Liam, mock-pouting.

Fayth patted his arm. 'You can break something else later.'

'Promise?'

'Long as it's yours and not mine.'

'What if it doesn't belong to either of us?'

'Then no. Can't have you ending up in jail. This year has been rough enough as it is.'

Liam stopped walking, his face dropping.

'I didn't mean it like that. I mean, not you.' She rubbed her hand over her face. That hadn't come out right. 'You're great. But a lot of shit has happened too. Astin's accident. Hollie and Astin breaking up. A crazy woman trying to kill us…'

Liam wrapped his arm around her waist and pulled her into him. 'But we have each other. We can get through anything so long as we have each other.'

'I know,' said Fayth, inhaling his cinnamon and sandalwood cologne. What would he do if they ever stopped making it? He wouldn't be him if he didn't smell like cinnamon and sandalwood.

She slipped her hand back into his and led him to where two pedicabs were waiting. Fayth and Liam hopped into the one at the front, while Wade climbed into the one behind them.

The driver remained quiet while Fayth and Liam

reminisced about the last time they'd been in New York together. Minus talk of Trinity. She spoiled enough already.

After a short ride, the pedicab driver pulled up near a hotdog stand. It wasn't the same one they'd been to before – that was somewhere else in the park – but it was lunchtime and she was starving.

She thanked and tipped the driver, then she, Liam, and Wade approached the stand as he drove off.

The smell of hotdogs and onions wafted through the air as they approached the stand. The man stood behind it was port with a beard that really should've been covered up. 'What'll it be?' he asked.

Liam was practically salivating beside her at the smell of hotdogs and onions. She glanced around. Wade was on high alert, as always. People walked past them without really paying any attention.

Liam nudged her.

'Hotdog with onions, please,' said Fayth. Her default hotdog order.

'Same please,' said Liam.

Fayth turned to Wade.

'Nothing for me, thanks. I had a big breakfast.'

'You're always hungry,' said Liam.

'There's always an exception to the rule.'

Liam was right – Wade *was* always hungry – but if he didn't want a hotdog, she wouldn't force him. She and Liam got their hotdogs and sat on the grass a few feet away. It was a bright, sunny day. Far brighter and sunnier than it should've been for October. If she'd still been in Scotland, it would've been in single digits and pissing it down. And everyone still would've been wearing t-shirts and shorts.

Wade rested against a tree nearby, glaring at anyone who gave Liam a second glance.

When she'd finished her hotdog, Fayth leaned back and looked up at the sky. It really was gorgeous out. Too bright for photos – unless they used Wade as a shield – but perfect for sitting back and relaxing.

'How was your hotdog?' said Fayth. If she was honest, she'd had better.

'It was OK,' said Liam.

'You hated it,' said Fayth.

'I didn't hate it, I just…do you feel a bit nauseous?'

'No. Wait. Yeah. A little. Oh no. You don't think it was the hotdog, do you?'

'Um, maybe. What did you have for breakfast?'

'Toast.' Her stomach made a gurgling noise. Acid rose up her oesophagus.

'Maybe we should go home just in case.'

'I don't think I can make it,' said Fayth, her stomach starting to rotate like a washing machine.

Liam gestured to Wade, who crouched down and joined them. 'What's up?'

So he hadn't been eavesdropping. That was good to know.

'Are there any restrooms nearby?' asked Liam.

'There are some around the corner,' said Wade.

'Desperate times,' said Fayth.

They made a beeline to the toilets, and luckily they were quiet. The bad things Fayth did in that toilet were not.

If the texts Liam sent to her while she stunk out the toilets were anything to go by, his stomach was in a similar position. Fayth spent the next half an hour recreating that scene from *Bridesmaids*. Some birthday that had turned out to be. Fucking typical. She'd tried to do something cute for him and it had completely backfired.

Her stomach calm enough for her to leave (or at least she hoped it was), she emerged from the safety of the toilets. They'd need to fumigate them if anyone was going to use them ever again.

Liam and Wade were outside, leaning against the wall, when she emerged. Liam looked as ill as she felt.

'I think we should go home,' said Liam.

'Yeah,' said Fayth with a sigh.

Liam took her hand and they walked as fast as they could back to Thalia.

'You're early,' said Thalia, putting a bookmark into her paperback as they climbed into the car.

'Don't ask,' said Fayth.

'Just get us home. Fast,' said Liam.

Thalia turned around to face them. They must've looked bad, because Thalia's face fell. 'Got it.'

She rushed them home. They made it back to the apartment, then Fayth had to run into the bathroom. Had they got food poisoning from that stall? God, she hoped not. That really would be fucking typical.

Weak and barely able to walk, Fayth crawled into the living room fifteen minutes later. Liam was sat on the sofa, hugging a washing-up bowl and channel hopping. Wade and Thalia stood a few feet away. They'd been joined by Ola, Liam's assistant, whose lips were pressed tightly together.

'Hey,' said Liam when he saw Fayth. His skin had a green tinge to it.

'Mmm,' said Fayth, not sure if she should speak. She was afraid that if she did, she might vomit again.

'Do you want some water?' offered Thalia.

'Mmm,' said Fayth.

'Come on, I'll help you into a chair,' said Wade. He did just that as Thalia and Ola got Fayth and Liam some water.

Ola returned with two pills. She handed one to Fayth, and one to Liam. 'Take these. They'll help.'

'What is it?' asked Liam.

'It stops the…erm…vomiting. And things.'

Fayth snatched it from Ola's hand and took it with a large swig of the water Thalia gave her. She'd take anything if it stopped the vomiting. She hadn't vomited like that since…ever. Ugh. She leaned back against the sofa. Her stomach was still doing swirlies.

Fucking hotdog.

*

Ola's magical tablets worked, and Fayth and Liam's stomachs calmed down. Thalia stayed over to babysit them anyway, unable to stop herself from mothering them. A part of Fayth was glad – Liam was a terrible patient and the last thing she needed was to look after him when she felt rough herself.

The next morning, she and Liam managed a couple of crackers for breakfast. 'I'm sorry,' said Fayth in between mouthfuls. She rested her elbows on the dining room table and put her head into her hands. The smaller she made herself, the less pain she was in.

'For what?' asked Liam.

'Ruining your birthday.'

Liam reached over and touched her hand. 'It wasn't you that ruined my birthday. It was those fucking hotdogs.'

'Which were my idea.'

'You were trying to be romantic. I get it.'

Fayth sighed. 'I just…I didn't know what to get you. You can literally go and buy whatever you want. What can I possibly give you that you can't buy yourself?'

Liam rubbed her hand. 'You. You're enough, Campbell. You always have been. You don't need to spend loads of money to impress me.' He kissed her hand.

Her stomach fluttered, but in a good way. How was he not pissed off at what had happened? She'd given him food poisoning! Well, not directly. But still.

*

Fayth and Liam spent the next few days mooching about on the sofa. Wade, Thalia, and Ola checked in regularly, as did Liam's cook and nutritionist. Fayth hid whenever his cook or nutritionist showed up, not to be rude, but because all talk of food just made her want to throw up again.

After a few days she upgraded from crackers to digestive biscuits and toast, but nothing appealed to her. She missed the psychological comfort food had often given her, but her body refused to shake the nausea. Liam seemed to bounce back much faster, and for that she was both grateful and jealous.

She was lying on the sofa curled in the foetal position when Ola walked in. 'Hey, you've got a parcel.' She handed an A4 envelope to Fayth.

Who would send her an A4 parcel? It couldn't be Hollie – clothes didn't fit in an A4 envelope.

Fayth sat up and opened the envelope. Inside was another envelope, and a note. She opened the note but didn't recognise the handwriting. Her eyes went straight to the signature. Astin.

Hey. Liam told me what happened. Hope you're feeling better. I found this online and thought of Liam. Don't tell him I found it, just say it's from you. Get well soon. Astin.

Fayth opened the other envelope. Inside was a first edition of the first issue of *The Amazing Spider-Man*. Just like the one Liam had had stolen by his stalker (and which the police were still holding on to as evidence).

Fayth reached across the coffee table for her phone and texted Astin to say thank you. The question was, why had he done it? Was he doing it because he was a good guy, or was he trying to get back on her good side?

Fayth took the magazine and note into the games room, where Liam was playing *World of Warcraft*. He flew his character – who was riding a griffin – onto the top of a building and turned to look at her. 'Hey, what's that?'

She handed the parcel to him. The note fell out as he pulled the comic from its envelope. 'Oh my god!' he kissed her, his face lit up like a Christmas tree.

'Don't thank me – Astin sent it.' Fayth picked up the

note and handed it to him.

He took a moment to read it, then said: 'Why didn't you say it was from you, like he suggested?'

'It felt wrong. He found it. He deserves credit. I don't get why he wouldn't want it.'

'Because it might look like he has an underlying motive?'

'What do you mean?'

'You're his ex-girlfriend's best friend. An ex-girlfriend whom he's still in love with, by the way. By helping you he proves to you he's not an asshole, but if he takes credit for it, it looks like he's doing it to look like a good guy and not because he genuinely is one.'

'That's a very complicated way of looking at things,' said Fayth.

'Yep,' agreed Liam, 'it is. Here's a simpler one: he doesn't feel like he deserves any credit and is trying to make things up to us after he was such a jerk.'

'I prefer the simpler version.'

Liam pulled her onto his lap. 'How are you feeling?'

'Mostly better. Still pissed off though. You?'

'I have Spider-Man. I'm happy.'

'Spider-Man makes you happy but I don't. I get it. I know where I stand.'

He kissed her cheek. 'You'll always come before Spider-Man. Just.'

Three

To make Fayth feel even more guilty for Liam getting food poisoning, he was due to go to LA and record the voiceover for an animated pirate dog film. Liam was super excited about it because he got to play the villain and didn't have to worry about looking pretty on camera.

He looked a little better, but he'd lost some weight from not eating. That didn't mean she wanted him to go, though. It would be the first time she'd been alone since their stalker had tried to kill them. Being around people she could just about pacify the fear, but when she was on her own the fear crept out like ants from under the porch.

'Are you sure you'll be all right?' Liam asked for the hundredth time as he stood by the door, ready to leave. Wade had already taken his bags to the car and was waiting downstairs.

'Yes, go,' said Fayth, hoping her poker face was better than it used to be.

'I'll only be gone for a week. Call me if you need anything. Thalia's happy to drive you anywhere, and I'm sure if you invited her for a drink she wouldn't say no either.'

'Isn't that weird? Going out with your driver?'

Liam shrugged. 'Is anything in our lives normal?'

'Not really,' said Fayth.

He kissed her forehead. 'Exactly. I'll see you in a few days.' He pressed his lips to hers in one final, lingering kiss. She wrapped her hands around his biceps, not wanting to let go. He'd been there for her through everything that had happened in the last few months, and she was terrified of what would happen if he left. But she couldn't stop him either. She wouldn't be *that* girlfriend. He pulled his lips away from hers, rested his head against hers for a moment, then left her. Alone. In a city full of guns just like the one that had given her a concussion.

Their stalker had broken into his previous apartment while he'd been away. She didn't know about his new one, but she had been his stalker. If anyone could find out about it, it was her. The pub had been in the middle of nowhere and she'd found that. The woman was resourceful, Fayth had to give her that.

Up until a couple of years ago, the Cock and Bull had been filled with mostly happy memories. Sure, there'd been arguments, but nothing crazy. Nothing life-altering. Not until she'd found out that her mum and sister had been in a car accident in the very kitchen where she was supposed to carry on working every day. After that, the pub had been forever tainted. Working there had never been the same.

Then, when their stalker had confronted them in the basement…

Fayth had walked down the stairs into the pub basement after a blackout. The fusebox was in there, and if she and Liam wanted to be able to see each other or make a drink, they needed the power back on. The light from her phone was pretty useless. Still, it was a simple fix. Or so she'd thought.

She'd pushed through the plastic curtain and rounded the corner. That's when she'd been hit with the gun.

BANG.

Fayth flinched. What was that? Was it a gun? Was someone outside, waiting for Liam? Was he OK? What if something happened to him? What if their stalker wasn't in jail back in Scotland like they'd been told, but she'd followed them back to New York?

She ran to the door, her hand hovering by the handle. What if Liam was outside, bleeding to death? No. That was silly. There was an armed doorman downstairs. But then, what if he was on their stalker's side? What if he was secretly out to get them, too?

She checked the door was locked, then backed away. She *had* to calm down. Practically running into the lounge, she closed all the doors then switched on the TV. That would help. She snuggled against the green leather, turning up the volume to drown out any outside sounds.

But then, what if someone came up behind her? If the TV was on too loud, she wouldn't hear it. They could knock her out and she wouldn't even get the chance to fight back. Just like last time.

She switched the TV off. She needed to stay alert. Staying alert was what would keep her alive.

It was hot. Way too hot. Even in baggy jeans and a t-shirt she was too warm. She should change into the shorts Hollie sent her. It was time she got over her complex about her legs. Liam liked them. She could learn to, couldn't she?

But if she went into the bedroom, she was farther away from the front door. If someone tried to break it down, how would she get out? Although if they broke in that way her escape route was blocked anyway.

A lump formed in her throat that was so big she could hardly swallow. What was *wrong* with her? When did she get so needy? She'd always loved being on her own. The last time she'd been in New York she'd wandered around alone loads while Hollie slept. How had she turned into a neurotic wreck in less than a year?

KNOCK KNOCK KNOCK.

Fayth screamed. Actually screamed. Her cheeks burned. It was just a knock at the door.

'Fayth? Is everything all right?' called Tate's singsong voice.

Fayth's body relaxed. It was just Tate. What was she

doing there?

She answered the door and let her friend in. Her skin was deeply tanned, no doubt from her recent holiday in Jamaica. If Fayth so much as looked at the sun her skin would turn crimson and her curly hair turned to cotton wool. Oh, to be able to pay someone else to worry about that stuff for you.

Tate turned to Fayth and narrowed her honey-coloured eyes. 'I've never seen your cheeks so red.'

'Um, thanks.'

'Do you need a glass of water?'

Water. Water was good. 'Yes. That's a good idea.' She led the way into the kitchen, perching on a stool while Tate got her a glass of water.

Tate sat beside her and handed her the glass. 'Did something happen after Liam left?'

Fayth sipped the water. 'No.'

'Are you sure?'

'Uh-huh.'

'Am I missing something?'

'Nope.'

'Fayth,' said Tate in that motherly way that she adopted when she was concerned.

Fayth raised the glass to her lips to take another sip, but the glass was already empty. She went over to the tap and refilled it. Tate watched her with narrowed eyes. The woman didn't know when to let things drop.

'I really am fine, Tate.'

'Promise me you'll never go into acting.'

'Oh you don't need to worry about that,' said Fayth. Her skin burned as if she'd been out in the sun all day. She hadn't even left the apartment yet.

'Should I call Hollie? Would that help?'

'No!' said Fayth. The last thing she needed was Hollie worrying about her. Hollie worried enough. If she gave Hollie any more to worry about she might just explode.

'Huh,' said Tate, tucking her blue hair behind her ear. How had she only just realised Tate's hair was blue? It was *blue* for crying out loud. That's not a subtle change from blonde.

'Is this to do with what happened at your pub?' said Tate.

Dammit.

'Have you been on your own since it happened?' probed Tate.

Fayth didn't answer. Tate already had her answers and she knew it.

'Why didn't you go with him?' asked Tate.

'I didn't want to miss out on my photography class,' said Fayth.

'When is it?'

'Wednesday.'

'Two days. All right. We should get some food in you. All that panic will have wreaked havoc with your blood sugar.'

Fayth snorted. 'I wasn't panicking.'

Tate glowered at her. 'To hell you weren't. I've had enough panic attacks to know what they look, feel, and sound like.' She straightened up, relaxing her facial muscles and turning them into a smile. 'There's this place around the corner that does great burgers if you're interested?'

'I thought you were vegan?'

'I thought you were a cook?' said Tate with a cheeky smirk. 'Vegan burgers are a thing too.'

'Touché,' said Fayth, 'but I'm sure you've got better things to do. You don't have to babysit me.'

'Actually,' said Tate, 'for the first time in months, my schedule is free. And it's not babysitting, it's hanging out with my friend. So what do you say?' She beamed at Fayth.

Fayth sighed. There was no way she could say no to Tate. She was too persuasive. And she was just trying to help. Her interference came from a good place. And was well-timed. Company wasn't such a bad idea, considering.

'All right,' said Fayth. 'Just let me go wash my face first.'

*

Fayth leaned back in the red leather chair, her empty plate sat on the table in front of her.

She, Tate, and Tate's latest bodyguard – who didn't say a word the whole time they were out, and barely seemed to acknowledge that they were there – had gone to a diner just around the corner. As much as Fayth hated to admit it, Tate was right – having something to eat had helped.

Tate smiled. 'Feel better?'

'Much,' said Fayth.

'Good.' Tate patted at the edges of her mouth with a napkin then placed it onto her plate. 'Do you want to talk about it?'

'Talk about what?' said Fayth. She glanced at Tate's bodyguard, who was sat next to Tate. His eyes were glued to the door, as if he expected someone threatening to walk in. His edginess made Fayth even more nervous.

Tate followed Fayth's gaze and shrugged. 'Whatever caused you to have a panic attack so bad it sounded like someone had attacked you.'

Fayth lowered her head. 'Was it really that bad?'

'Yeah,' said Tate. She reached out and touched Fayth's arm. It offered Fayth a little comfort. She loved Liam, but she needed a friend, too, and with him gone she didn't have anyone. She couldn't talk to Maisie about everything – she hadn't known her long enough. Tate knew most things already, and everything else she'd already figured out. But Fayth couldn't talk about it. Just thinking about what had happened in the pub's basement made her want to throw her burger up all over the table.

'Have you considered talking to someone?'

'I'm talking to you. Kind of.'

'Someone with more experience than me.'

Fayth slumped. 'Oh. You mean a counsellor.' She had nothing against counsellors, but she didn't like the idea of going to one. Why would she go to a total stranger and tell them everything? How would that be any easier than talking to Hollie or her sister?

'Don't say it like that. It's not like that. It helps, honest.'

Fayth pursed her lips. 'Even if I wanted to, it'd be months – maybe even years – before I could see someone. The waitlist in big cities to see someone is ridiculous. It's even worse in rural areas. I don't even know if our local area *has* any counsellors. Even if they did, I'm not suicidal, so they won't rush me through.' Fayth sighed. 'Not to mention I want to do more travelling, and there's no way I can see a counsellor regularly if I'm travelling.' She had all the reasons in the world not to see a counsellor, but deep down, somewhere at the very, very back of her mind, she knew that she needed one.

Tate opened her clutch, took out a business card, and handed it to Fayth. 'I've seen Dr Kaur for, I don't know, five years now? She's amazing. I think she could really help you. She does video consultations too.' Of course Tate had all the counterarguments. Tate had an answer for everything.

'You want me to pay to speak to someone?'

'It's not cheap, I know, but wouldn't your alternative back home be to go private anyway?'

Fayth ground her teeth. Damn Tate always being right.

'What's more important? Your money or your health?' said Tate.

Fayth ran her hands through her ponytail. More strands fell out as she pulled her hand away. Her hair had been falling out for months. She couldn't shake the nausea, and some days she'd wake up with a headache so bad she wouldn't be able to function until the paracetamol had kicked in. She'd spoken to her GP and gone for some blood tests before leaving for New York, but they'd come back clear. The doctor had asked her if anything was bothering her, but she'd lied. The doctor knew her family and knew what had happened, but he didn't push her. But how much longer could she keep lying to herself? How much longer could she keep fooling herself and pretending she was all right when it was obvious to everyone that she wasn't?

*

Fayth stayed at Tate's apartment that night. She hadn't planned to, but they'd fallen asleep watching *Heathers*. When Fayth returned to Liam's apartment the following morning, she was still on edge but not as much. Tate wasn't far away, but Fayth didn't want to burden her any more than she already had. Tate had her own problems to worry about.

She checked the door was locked a couple of times, then stuck a stool from the kitchen behind it just in case. Nobody was due to cook or clean, so she could leave that there until the morning when Liam's cleaner came in. Nobody would ever have to know it was there.

She took Dr Kaur's business card from her coat pocket and twirled it around her fingers. She had to call. She knew she had to call. But if she did, she'd have to talk to Dr Kaur about everything that had happened to her, and she wasn't ready to bring all of that back up. She'd buried it deep in the ocean of her mind and it needed to stay there. Except it wouldn't. It crept up – often at night – and disturbed her sleep. She woke up in cold sweats, the faces of her mum, sister, ex-husband, stalker, and Trinity flashing through her mind. It was a miracle she hadn't woken Liam up with her nightmares.

How did Hollie deal with her insomnia? She'd suffered for years. She must've developed some sort of coping mechanism. Fayth could ask her. Then she wouldn't have to go to therapy. Or would she? And would asking Hollie for advice on a subject like that make Hollie worry even more?

Hollie had seen a counsellor in the past and sworn by it,

saying how much it had helped her in her darkest moments. Was Fayth at that point too?

She sunk onto the green leather sofa and stared at the card. It was white, with *Dr Kaur* on one line, *Psychiatrist* on another, and a phone number on a third. That was it. It was a good use of white space.

And she was procrastinating.

Sighing, she stood up and retrieved her phone from the bedroom. Doing the right thing wasn't always the easiest choice, but what was the alternative? Spend the rest of her life terrified of being alone?

Four

'Good morning all!' said Jasper. He sounded even more chipper than usual. 'Welcome to Central Park!' He grinned, his arms wide open and his camera dangling from around his neck. 'Thank you all for meeting me here. Since the weather's so good, I thought we'd work on some outdoor photography this week.' He looked up at the sky. 'We'll split up and take some shots now, meet back up in a couple of hours, have some lunch, then take some more photos if the weather is still good. If we've got time at the end, we'll talk through them, if not we'll do it next week.' He talked to them for a little while longer, then they went their separate ways. Fayth and Maisie were walking off when they heard Liesel and Arthur arguing.

'You carry it then!' cried Liesel.

'I can't! My back's gone!' said Arthur.

Fayth and Maisie exchanged glances.

Maisie turned around. 'Do you need any help carrying stuff?' she offered. 'This stuff's pretty awkward.'

'No,' said Liesel.

Arthur ignored her. 'Yes please.'

Liesel rolled her eyes. She could be grumpy at times, but it was clear from the way she looked at Arthur that she loved him.

Maisie took Arthur's bag while Fayth took Liesel's. The four of them then set off to find a spot where they could take some photos. Fayth was conscious of not walking too far or too fast, but Liesel and Arthur did a pretty good job of keeping up considering their ages.

'How about here?' suggested Fayth as they arrived at the edge of some trees. 'The trees should offer some good shade.'

'I like it,' said Arthur, nodding. He rested his hand on his hip, his face distorted in pain. Poor guy.

'It'll do,' said Liesel.

Maisie put the bags on the floor and began to set up a tripod. 'Who wants to go first?'

'Fayth should since it was her idea,' said Arthur.

'Agreed,' said Maisie.

'All right,' said Fayth. 'I want to take a photo of you two.'

Liesel frowned.

'Please?' said Fayth in her sweetest voice.

'Fine,' said Liesel.

Fayth directed Liesel and Arthur to a spot in front of the trees and took some photos using depth of focus to stop the detail of the leaves from distracting from Liesel and Arthur. She used the tripod for some, lay on the floor for others, and for the last couple, stood on a tree trunk. Those were her favourites: she got both their vulnerability and their affection for one another.

The other three took some photos there too, then they moved on and tried out a few more locations. Before long, it was time to meet back up with the rest of the group for lunch. They'd each brought something for the picnic, so they sat and tried out everyone's dishes. While it wasn't a hot, sunny day, it was a pleasant autumnal day. Everyone talked and laughed. Even Rupert chimed in from time to time. Fayth felt more relaxed than she had for a while.

Until she heard someone shout her name.

The hairs on the back of her neck stood up. Who was it?

She turned. A group of a dozen or so people holding cameras were running towards them. Paparazzi.

'Fuck,' she said without even thinking. 'Sorry.'

'Are you famous or something?' said Marisol, lowering

her sunglasses.

'Or something,' said Fayth. The paparazzi were a couple of hundred yards away at most. Fayth began to pack up her things. 'I need to go.'

'Of course,' said Jasper.

'I'm so sorry.'

'It's not your fault,' said Jasper.

The rest of the group stayed silent. Rupert's face was tense. That guy really needed to remove the stick from his arse.

Maisie began to pack up too. 'My place isn't far. You can hide out there.'

'Thanks,' said Fayth. She had no time to argue.

'Fayth! Fayth! What do you think of the single?' a paparazzo called as they were a few feet away.

Single? What single?

Whatever. It didn't matter. She could figure that out later. Right now, she needed to get away before they swarmed her like a pack of dogs. Fayth and Maisie finished shoving their things into their bags as the paparazzi reached them. They swarmed Fayth and her friends like flies around rotting flesh.

'Do you *mind?*' said Liesel. 'We're trying to have a quiet lunch here.'

The paparazzi ignored her and continued to descend on Fayth. Their cameras flashed away.

'How does it feel to be thrust into the spotlight from nowhere?' shouted a paparazzo.

Terrible. She much preferred nowhere.

Fayth spotted an empty pedicab a few feet away. She tapped Maisie's arm. They ran for it, calling out to the driver. Thankfully, he noticed what was going on, stopped, and ushered them onboard.

'I can't leave the park,' he said, 'but I'll take you as far as I can.'

'Thanks,' said Fayth.

The paparazzi were on foot – they'd never catch up. Or

at least, not until they found another pedicab to ride.

When they were finally out of sight of the flashbulbs, Fayth had to ask the driver: 'Why'd you help us?'

'I've seen people get swarmed before. It's not nice,' said the pedicab driver.

'No, it's not,' said Fayth. She could still count on one hand how many times it had happened to her, but it was still far too many. Liam had always told her he preferred New York to LA because there were fewer paparazzi. She was starting to wonder if he'd just said that to make her feel better.

What spin would the press put on the photos this time? Would they call her boring? Unsociable? Rude? It wouldn't be the first time she'd been called all of the above. Or worse.

Maybe they wouldn't be able to sell the photos because there was no story to go with them and no Liam. That was her favourite option. And the least likely.

*

The pedicab took them to the edges of the park, then they ran to Maisie's apartment. It was a small apartment in a run-down building, but it was exactly how Fayth had expected Maisie's apartment to look: shabby chic.

'Thanks again,' said Fayth when they were safely inside. 'I owe you.'

'Don't worry about it,' said Maisie. 'I don't get celebrity culture. Do you want some tea? I have camomile, peppermint, or red bush.'

That wasn't tea to Fayth, but she accepted a camomile anyway. She'd had camomile before, and she didn't hate it. It still wasn't as good as normal tea, but it would do. It would soothe her. Or she hoped it would.

'I thought all the attention had died down,' said Fayth, sinking onto a beanbag while Maisie poured hot water into a teapot.

'What do you mean?' said Maisie.

'I thought people were getting bored of us,' said Fayth with a sigh.

Maisie handed her a teacup and sat on a beanbag beside her. 'Could it be because of Trinity's new single? I mean, people seem to be adamant it's about you two. They're probably after some sort of reaction.'

'What? When did that come out?'

'I'm not sure. It's everywhere, though,' said Maisie.

Marvellous. Suddenly she couldn't face a cup of tea. Or any form of sustenance, for that matter. She felt sick. Really sick. Almost as bad as she had when she'd eaten those fucking hotdogs. 'And it's definitely about us?'

'She hasn't confirmed it, but everyone seems pretty certain. They probably want to gauge your reaction. It's called *The Sinner*. I hate to say it, but it's a hell of a power ballad.'

Sigh.

'How do you know all this?'

'My sister mentioned Trinity Gold had a new single out and that it was about her ex. I was curious, so I did some digging.'

Fayth put her tea down and curled up in the beanbag. 'I just wish they'd leave me alone. I'm really not that interesting.'

Maisie snorted. 'You're good at selling yourself short, though.'

'Well it's true. I'm *not* interesting compared to someone like Trinity. I'm like beige next to fuchsia.'

'Trinity seems like the kind of larger-than-life character that makes everyone seem bland.'

'Exactly. Liam and Tate are the only ones I know who can keep up with her.'

'Tate?'

'Tate Gardener.'

Maisie shook her head, her expression blank.

'Wow, you really do live under a rock. Didn't you watch any TV when you were younger?'

'Not really. My head was always in a book. Is she friend or foe?'

'Friend. She's helping Hollie with her fashion business. She used to be Trinity's best friend but Trinity blacklisted her for reasons I still don't get.'

'Hollywood is so fickle,' said Maisie.

'Isn't it?'

Five

Liam had only been gone for a week, but it felt like a whole lot longer. Fayth had never been dependent on anyone, and she didn't like it. Even when her ex-husband had gone on a lads' holiday she hadn't missed him that much. Then again, he was an arsehole. Liam was one of the good guys. And it wasn't like she'd put her life on hold for him while he'd been gone. She'd even made steps to try to be fully functioning again by booking an appointment with Dr Kaur.

She wasn't sure how he'd react to her finally deciding to go. He'd suggested it before, but telling him still made her nervous. Sure, he'd been to rehab, but that was different. He'd been an addict. For the most part, she was stable. Wasn't she?

She lay back on the sofa and stretched. A couple of days earlier she'd found some weights in the games room and had started using them. Big mistake. It'd only been just over a month since the pub had closed, but her muscles were already opposed to heavy lifting. She was seriously out of practise.

The front door opened.

'Where's my favourite photographer hiding?'

Fayth suppressed a giggle. So cheesy.

The living room door opened and he walked in, grinning. He walked over and kissed her cheek. 'Were you asleep?'

'Just stretching,' she said. 'This thing's comfy.'

'Much comfier than a plane,' he said, lifting her feet up,

sitting down, and lying her feet across his lap.

'You have a private jet,' said Fayth. 'You only get to complain if you fly economy.'

'Doesn't mean I like travelling. So, what's new? What did I miss?'

'You make it sound like you expect loads to have happened while you were gone.'

'It's New York. There's always loads going on.'

There it was. Her opening to say something.

Gulp.

'What?'

'So after you left, I kind of…I think I had a panic attack.'

The colour drained from Liam's face.

'I'm fine now, but Tate came over just after you left and she found me and she suggested I speak to someone.'

'Dr Kaur?'

'How'd you guess?'

'Tate's been seeing her for years. She's pretty well-known in Hollywood.'

Of course she was. 'Have you seen her? That might be weird.'

'No, but I've heard good things.' He pulled her into a hug. 'I'm sorry for leaving you. If I'd known—'

'No, it's OK. I'm OK. It's helped to put things into perspective. I can't carry on how I am.'

He kissed her forehead. 'You know you can talk to me, right?'

'I know. But you also know it's not the same.'

He nodded, pulling her even closer. They sat quietly for a moment. It was the first time Fayth had felt relaxed since he'd gone. Was that how it was supposed to be in a relationship? Was that how someone who actually cared about you was supposed to make you feel?

'Come on,' said Liam, leading her into the kitchen and switching on the kettle. 'Alexa, put the radio on,' he said. His Amazon Echo – which Fayth had forgot was even there –

introduced the radio station, then NSYNC's *Pop* began to blare through its speakers. Boy bands were never really her thing, but she couldn't deny how catchy the song was. Liam started bopping along, a cheeky grin on his face. Fayth shook her head but couldn't control her giggles. He grabbed her hand and spun her around a few times. Still laughing, she lost her footing and stumbled. She went sideways on her ankle. Liam grabbed her before she could hit the floor. 'You all right?' he said.

'Yep,' she replied, lifting her ankle and massaging it. It throbbed a bit, but she'd done worse. She'd be fine.

And then the song changed.

It wasn't a song Fayth recognised, but the voice was all too familiar.

Trinity.

Fayth froze. Liam didn't seem to notice. Didn't he know who it was? He had to. He knew her better than anyone. Not to mention she had a distinct, husky voice. She was a good singer and songwriter, there was no denying that (sadly). But that didn't change that the song was about them.

'We had everything, you and me,

but it wasn't mean to be.

I sinned and you couldn't forgive me,

I hurt you and you couldn't forgive me,

I lost you and I can't forgive myself.

You moved on to someone you thought better

Does she make you happier, stronger, wetter?

What does she offer that I don't?

What does she do that I won't?'

Those were some serious lyrics, that was for sure. If they weren't about her and Liam, she might've been able to fully appreciate them. As it was, every time Fayth listened to them, she pictured Trinity's smug face twisting a knife into a voodoo doll while her entourage and hoards of fans laughed in the background. Ugh.

'What's wrong?' said Liam.

The kettle finished boiling, but neither of them moved.

'Doesn't it bother you that Trinity wrote a song about us?'

He shrugged.

'Seriously?'

'You think it's the first song she's written about me?'

She'd never thought about that…

'Half her last album was about me. She's a songwriter. It's what she does. It's no different than you writing poetry about Patrick.'

'Yes it is!'

'Why is it?'

'Because nobody reads my poetry! The whole fucking world hears Trinity slag us off!'

'Everyone knows it's bullshit,' said Liam.

'Do they?' said Fayth. 'Is that why Twitter is full of people threatening all sorts because we've hurt Trinity? Isn't her talking crap how we ended up with a stalker in the first place?' Fayth stormed out of the room and into the living room. What was wrong with him? Why didn't it bother him?

Unfortunately, he followed her. 'I'm sorry, Campbell. I didn't think about it like that.'

He reached out to her, but she stepped away from him.

'You may be immune to the horrible things that people say, but I'm not,' said Fayth.

Of course he was immune to it – he'd grown up with it. She'd grown up in a bubble that had only recently been burst.

He leaned against the back of the sofa. 'What do you want me to say? I can't make people stop. I wish I could.'

'I know,' she said, pacing the living room. 'But with that song she's brought it all back. I was just starting to move on, and she's gone and—' Fayth's eyes filled with tears. She didn't have the energy to stop herself from crying. She fell onto the sofa and started bawling. Trinity, the song, the flashbacks, the stalker, the pub, Patrick, her mum, her sister…it was all too much. Too much had changed and gone wrong in the last eighteen months and she hadn't had a chance to stop and process any of it. When would she get a chance to process it all? When would she get a break?

'I'm sorry,' said Liam. He pulled her into a hug, and this time she didn't resist. 'I didn't realise it was this bad.'

Fayth snorted. 'Yeah. Well. I'm a better liar than I think.'

NOVEMBER

One

Dr Kaur was a petite woman with a warm smile. She wasn't cold or clinical like Fayth had expected. She greeted Fayth with a handshake, then pointed to a chair where Fayth could sit down. The small room was sparse, with a handful of landscapes hung on the cream walls.

'So,' said Dr Kaur. 'Today we'll do an assessment, then we'll work out a plan. How long did you say you're in New York for?'

'Until just before Christmas.'

Dr Kaur scribbled something into her notebook. 'If you want to continue after that, we can talk over the phone or video chat if you like.'

'Thanks.' That wouldn't be necessary, but Fayth didn't want to be rude. She just needed a couple of sessions to work through her issues with being alone, that was all.

'Tell me, what's your family life like?' asked Dr Kaur.

Her family life? She hadn't expected that question.

'I…' She clasped her forehead as a sharp pain shot through her head. Her mouth went so dry she could barely speak or swallow. Her brain picked the perfect time to forget how to form words.

'Would you like some water?' offered Dr Kaur.

Fayth nodded, not sure if the words would come out. Dr Kaur left her alone for a moment, then returned with a glass of water. 'Thank you,' squeaked Fayth. She took a few sips. Her throat loosened a little.

'Did something happen to your family?' asked Dr Kaur.

Fayth finished the glass of water, then she began to talk. And once she started, she couldn't stop.

'Do you ever suffer from nausea or headaches? An upset stomach?' asked Dr Kaur after Fayth had spent most of the session explaining her familial situation and her former marriage.

'Sometimes, yeah.' More like all the time.

'What about breakouts? Does your hair fall out in clumps? Do your muscles ache for no reason?'

'Are you psychic?'

Dr Kaur laughed. 'No. They're all physical symptoms of stress. There are many more.'

Fayth slumped in her chair. Could it really do that much damage?

'Just as there are hundreds of physical symptoms of PMS and they differ from person to person, the symptoms of long-term stress do, too. A little stress in the short-term can help how we perform in tasks, but long-term stress can also cause memory problems, eczema, even strokes.'

Fayth blinked, not fully processing what Dr Kaur was saying. 'What?'

'What triggers stress varies from person to person,' continued Dr Kaur. 'It's how we, as an individual, perceive a situation. Some people thrive in exam environments, for example. Others stress themselves out so much that even someone as young as sixteen can have a stroke.'

Fayth widened her eyes. A stroke? At *sixteen*? Was she at risk of having a stress-induced stroke?

'We often don't realise the impact our environment and moods can have on our body. We assume it can't have a psychological cause, but it often does.'

'Shite,' said Fayth, leaning back in the squishy chair. 'Sorry,' she added. Were you allowed to swear in therapy?

'That's OK, you can say whatever you like in here without censorship.'

'Thanks.'

'What did you think was causing your physical symptoms?'

'I don't know,' said Fayth. 'A couple of people had suggested some things could be stress, but I didn't think they could *all* be that.' Fayth ran her hand through her hair. She really had to stop picking up Liam's mannerisms; if she lost any more strands of hair she was going to start going bald. 'When I got my divorce papers through I chucked up and was ill for a bit, but I assumed it was a stomach bug that my body just couldn't fight off.'

'I see,' said Dr Kaur. 'It can weaken our immune system and make us more prone to picking up bugs, but after a period of long-term stress, when we perceive that stress to be over, it's not uncommon for our body to purge. Getting your divorce papers through was the last page of a very long chapter in your life. It's no wonder your body couldn't handle it.'

'I hate my body,' mumbled Fayth.

'Why?'

'For all the reasons you listed above. I feel like it's working against me right now and I don't know how to fix it.'

Dr Kaur tucked her pen behind her ear and rested her hands in her lap. 'Isn't that why you're here?'

*

Fayth continued on with the rest of the week, but Dr Kaur's words stuck with her. Her mental health was worse than she'd thought. Then class had turned out even worse than her first lesson when she was forced to work with Rupert again. As he always did when they worked together, he ignored her. He refused to take her direction and took the most unflattering photos of her imaginable. A part of her wanted to say something to Jasper, but a stronger part of her didn't want to be *that* person. What could Jasper do anyway?

It was Rupert's money that was being wasted if he didn't want to learn.

Things didn't improve at the end when Jasper informed them that the following week they had to bring a guest.

'Class not go so well today?' Liam asked as Fayth walked into the living room.

Fayth threw her bag onto the chair by the door and sunk onto the sofa beside him. 'I have to take a friend in next week.'

'Why?' he asked, stroking her hair as she curled up beside him. The smell of Liam's cologne offered her some comfort after a long few days.

'Because Jasper said so.' Fayth sighed. 'Who am I supposed to take? All my friends outside of that class and in New York are celebrities.'

'So?' said Liam.

She raised her head to look at him. 'So I can't just take you or Tate to a class like that!'

'Why not?'

'Because you're you!'

'That's not a reason. We are people too, you know. We're pretty good on camera, too,' said Liam.

'You twitch whenever someone tries to take your photo,' Fayth reminded him.

'Accidentally on purpose,' he corrected with a sly grin.

'So…you'd do it?'

'Of course I would. Why wouldn't I?' He kissed her forehead.

'I didn't think you'd want to,' she said.

'I'd do anything for you,' he said, kissing the tip of her nose.

'Would you wear a silly hat?'

'Depends how silly.' He kissed her cheek.

'I don't know. You don't have to wear one. At least I don't think you do, anyway.'

'I draw the line at anything that involves tassels.' He

kissed her other cheek.

'Noted. Now will you kiss me properly please?'

He grinned, leaning forwards and finally kissing her lips. Electricity shot through her. He had a way of making her feel better just by being there. When he kissed her, well, that helped even more. He ran his fingers through her hair, pulling her closer. Their lives weren't perfect, and they had a lot of issues to work through, but Liam was exactly the kind of person she needed.

*

'It seems like you have a lot of pent-up anger at Trinity,' said Dr Kaur at therapy the following week. It was nearing the end of the session, and Fayth had spent most of it ranting about Trinity. Pent-up anger was an understatement.

Fayth snorted. 'That's one way of putting it.'

'How else would you put it?'

'She's the root cause of most of my recent problems, and she refuses to acknowledge it! She won't even listen when I try to reason with her!'

'Have you tried?'

'I've…attempted…I think…' Had she, though, or had she just lost her temper almost every time the topic of Trinity was brought up, let alone when she was faced with her? Fayth sunk further into her chair. 'Or not.'

'Do you think it would help you if you did?'

Fayth crossed her arms over her chest. 'I don't know. It's not like she's a big fan of listening.'

'But perhaps trying to have a civil conversation with her, if nothing else, would at least give you some closure,' said Dr Kaur, resting her arms on her clipboard.

Was it closure that she needed, or was it something else? Fayth wasn't sure any more. Dr Kaur did have a point, though – perhaps it was time to try to have a civil conversation with Trinity. She'd reached out to her for a reason. Would she still be interested in meeting up? There was only one way to find out.

Two

While Fayth still wasn't sure meeting Trinity was a good idea, Liam arranged for them to meet later in the week at a cafe in Brooklyn. In the meantime, Fayth had photography class to distract her.

She was still terrified of taking Liam to class, but he insisted it was fine and even seemed excited to join her. His support was cute, and she was completely not used to it. Patrick had always just left her to whatever she was doing. The only thing he encouraged her to do was cook, but if she dared to cook anything unusual, he'd wrinkle his nose. Oh, how things change.

Fayth and Liam were some of the first to arrive during guest week. Marisol stood at the back, talking to her guest – a woman about her age – about the different parts of the photography set ups. They smiled and waved at Fayth and Liam, then returned to their conversations. Just the kind of reaction Fayth liked from people.

Maisie and her friend were stood by the window, staring out. They both wore thick, woollen sweaters that Fayth had no doubt Maisie had made herself, as she was an avid knitter. Fayth really needed to get back into knitting herself. She'd always found it soothing. Fayth and Liam walked over to join them.

'Hey,' said Fayth.

'Hi!' said Maisie, turning around and hugging Fayth. 'This is my friend Violet.'

Violet stared at Liam, her fuchsia lips agape. Maisie

closed her mouth. 'Sorry. I did try to prepare her. She's a big *Highwater* fan.'

'Omigod. It's you. It's like, really you. How can it be you?' cried Violet.

Liam chuckled. Violet's legs practically gave way. Maisie clung to her to steady her.

'It's good to meet you,' said Liam, holding his hand out to her.

Her eyes wide, she reached out and shook his hand, then retracted her hand and stared at it. 'Liam York just shook my hand!' she squealed to Maisie.

'What did we say about fangirling?' said Maisie.

Liam chuckled. 'It's fine, don't worry about it.'

'Sorry,' said Violet, her voice returning to normal.

Thank god he didn't have a catchphrase.

Rupert entered, a girl who looked to be about six in tow. Shouldn't she be at school? When he noticed Liam, his nostrils flared. He turned away. The girl with him noticed Liam and her eyes widened. She tugged on his shirt repeating *'Daaaaaad'* in that way only little girls can over and over. Rupert ignored her, settling on a couple of seats as far away from them as possible. Fayth turned away. The less she thought about Rupert, the better.

'Mommy would let me!' the girl shouted at Rupert.

Ouch. His face filled with a combination of anger and heartbreak. He fiddled with the rim of his cap. The buzzing room fell to an eery silence.

'Olivia—'

The girl curled her hands into fists, turned on her heels, and stormed out of the room. Rupert charged after her, barging past an oblivious Jasper as he entered the room. Jasper shot him a confused glance, then returned to his usual chipper demeanour. 'Good morning! And welcome to our guests! I've brought some stickers so that we don't get embarrassed if we forget anyone's names. Come up and help yourselves when you're ready.'

Rupert returned to the room, his daughter dragging her feet behind him. Her face was scrunched up and her fingers were frantically plaiting her long, chestnut hair.

Fayth went up to get stickers for the four of them. Rupert sidled up beside her as his daughter relocated to the back of the room. Fayth ripped off four stickers from the strip.

'Wouldn't have thought your boyfriend needs one,' said Rupert.

Pretending she hadn't heard him, Fayth returned to her friends. What *was* his problem, exactly?

'Everything all right?' said Liam.

Fayth relaxed her features. She hadn't realised how tense she was. 'Mmm.'

Rupert? Maisie mouthed.

Fayth nodded.

Maisie rolled her eyes. *Cock*.

Fayth laughed. Yes, yes he was.

*

Guest week went better than Fayth had expected. Rupert was as abrasive as ever, but everyone else was as warm towards Liam as they were towards the rest of the group. To them, he was just her guest. Liam seemed to enjoy being treated like everyone else, but it was always hard to tell with him because it was so easy for him to hide things.

Still, it had been a fun day. Fayth had taken some amazing photos of Liam if she didn't mind saying so herself, then they'd all gone out for drinks afterwards. It was such a great day she forgot all about her meeting with Trinity.

Until the following morning, when there were just twenty-four hours to go until she met with her arch nemesis. Was meeting up with that sociopath really a good idea? Dr Kaur had been right about other things. And since therapy was costing her a small fortune, she had to try. Right?

The day before meeting with Trinity dragged on. Fayth

tortured herself by listening to *The Sinner*, even going as far as watching the music video, which featured two people who looked *a lot* like Fayth and Liam. Fayth had no doubt that if the characters in it had spoken, the Fayth lookalike would've had a Scottish accent.

Liam noticed what she was doing and distracted her with some raids on *World of Warcraft*, then they fell asleep on the sofa watching Brendan Fraser in *The Mummy*. When Fayth awoke the next morning, every bone in her body protested. It was as if her body was trying to tell her not to meet with that lunatic. But it was too late to back out.

To give her some moral support without taking someone who would provoke a reaction (like Liam or Tate), Wade went with her to meet Trinity.

'You all right, Scot?' asked Wade as they walked down the busy street to the cafe where they'd agreed to meet.

'Terrific,' said Fayth.

Wade stopped. 'Nobody's forcing you to do this. Say the word and we can go right back.'

'No, it's fine,' said Fayth. 'I need to do this.'

'OK, it's your call.' Wade started walking again. Fayth followed. He was right, of course. Nobody *was* forcing her to talk to Trinity. But Fayth needed to know why Trinity had released that song about her and brought back all of those memories. Why Trinity had such a vendetta against her. Why she'd sabotaged any hope of Hollie and Astin reconciling at Tate's charity gala. Why she was such a bitch.

Wade cleared his throat. 'It's here,' he said, pointing to a cafe she'd just walked past.

'Oh, thanks.' Fayth turned back around and went inside, Wade close behind her. The cafe was dingy and dark, and it reeked of grease more than any chippy Fayth had ever set foot in. It was the last place Fayth would've expected someone like Trinity to hang out in. Was that the point?

A guy a little smaller than Wade sat at the grubby bar in the centre of the room. Wade approached him and man-hugged him. 'Hey man, long time.'

'Yeah. Hands are pretty full right now,' he said, jerking his head towards someone sat in the corner. Their hood was up and their back was to the door. Was that Trinity? Fayth's body tensed.

'Fayth, this is Byron, Trinity's bodyguard,' said Wade.

'You have my condolences,' said Fayth, shaking his hand.

Byron chuckled. 'She's pretty calm right now.'

'I'm sure that will change when she sees me,' said Fayth.

'You do seem to have that effect on her,' said Wade. 'Want a drink?'

'Vodka?' said Fayth, only half-joking.

Wade chuckled. 'Not sure it's that kind of place. Lemonade do?'

'I suppose,' she said with a sigh.

'All right, I'll get it sent over. Good luck.'

'Thanks,' said Fayth.

She approached the figure sat in the corner and slid into the seat opposite. Trinity looked up. Her eyes were gaunt, her olive skin drained of colour. She'd lost some weight, but she was still buxom. For once, though, she was completely covered up. Her black hoody was zipped up to the top, the hood covering most of her hair with the exception of a few stray strands. Her bloodshot eyes were framed with purple bags and her skin was blotchier than a tie-dyed t-shirt. Was this the face of Trinity Gold without make-up and without pretence?

If it was, it was even scarier than Trinity in full regalia. This wasn't Trinity in Hollywood mode: this was Trinity in normal-person mode. Who knew Trinity even knew how to be normal?

A waiter placed a glass of water in front of Trinity and a lemonade in front of Fayth, then walked off. Fayth glanced over at Wade and Byron. Their eyes were fixed on Fayth and Trinity. She gave them a sheepish smile. Trinity still hadn't spoken. She'd requested the meeting, yet she didn't seem to want to speak first.

The silence was excruciating. There was no music playing in the background of the cafe. The only sound came from the hissing of the coffee machine and the handful of other customers talking. It was almost too quiet. Would someone notice if they got into an argument? Would it end up in the gossip blogs if they did? Was that why Trinity had chosen somewhere so quiet?

Trinity picked up her glass of water and sipped. Then – finally – she spoke: 'I wanted to apologise.'

Fayth blinked a few times. She wanted to what now?

'I think we got off on the wrong foot.'

Understatement, much?

'You know, I'm really not as bad as you think I am.'

Did Trinity have a twin no one knew about? That was the only way to explain the direction the conversation was going in.

'Why is that?' asked Fayth.

Trinity rubbed her red nose with the back of her hand. 'Well, I mean, I like, I help people. I'm nice to people.'

Fayth resisted the urge to laugh. 'You broke up Hollie and Astin. Intentionally. Then you got them into an argument so bad that they're still not speaking three months later. You betrayed Liam by doing drugs in his club, despite knowing he was a recovering addict himself. You announced that the two of you had broken up in front of the entire crowd at HighCon. Oh, and you released a song about us.'

Trinity studied her nails for a few moments. 'Look, I never said I was perfect.'

'Are you saying you didn't change the seating arrangements at Tate's charity gala to put Hollie and Astin next to one another?'

'I thought talking it out might do them some good.'

'And that's why you mentioned their break-up before the starter, was it?'

'I never said timing was my strong point.' The door

opened. Trinity's back stiffened. When she saw the reflection of an old couple enter in the mirror on the opposite wall, she relaxed.

'Is that why you announced your break-up with Liam so publicly?' said Fayth.

'The fans had a right to know!'

Fayth snorted. 'No they didn't. Nobody has the right to the details of someone else's personal life.'

'That's not how it works in Hollywood, babe.'

'Don't call me babe,' growled Fayth. 'I'm not a sheep-pig.'

'A what?'

'Never mind,' said Fayth. 'Just because someone is a part of Hollywood that doesn't mean they have to share everything about their lives. I'll bet even the Kardashians don't share everything.'

'No, that's true,' agreed Trinity, 'but I'm not a Kardashian. I'm a songwriter. I tell my truth in my songs. It's not my fault if people don't like it.'

'Don't like it? We're getting rape and death threats because of that bloody song. Someone tried to kill us because of your bloody songs and social media posts!'

Trinity giggled. It turned into a retching, hacking cough. Blood appeared on the back of her hand. Fayth passed her a couple of serviettes from the dispenser on the table. She snatched them from Fayth, wiped her nose, then replied: 'It's not my fault my fans are loyal.'

'You call that loyalty? Most people would call that psychopathy.'

Trinity shrugged.

'You don't get it, do you?' said Fayth.

'Get what?'

Fayth sighed. 'Why am I even bothering?' She'd had better conversations with her dogs.

'You want to know why I released that song,' said Trinity. For once, she was right.

'Are you going to tell me?'

Trinity sighed. 'I wrote that months ago. The record label agreed it was good. It's nothing personal.'

'Why do you not get it? Of course it's fucking personal! Everyone *knows* it's about us!'

'But I haven't said that.'

'You have models who look like Liam and me in the video. You practically did a *Cry Me a River*.'

'You know, I did cover that in one of my shows not long after the break-up—'

'Not the point. You intentionally made it obvious the song is about us.'

'No, I didn't,' said Trinity. 'It's just a marketing thing. People love a good bit of drama. They love it even more if it's real. Or at least, what they think is real. Like I said – it's nothing personal.'

'I swear to god if you say that one more time.'

'You'll what?' Trinity smirked. 'We're in a public place. And my bodyguard is here.'

Fayth was pretty sure Byron wouldn't stop her if she lunged for Trinity. He was too engrossed in his catch-up with Wade anyway. 'Do you ever consider how other people will feel before you do something?'

'Of course I do!'

'Uh-huh. So then why'd you release a song about Liam and me without warning us?'

'Oh please! You think this is the first song I've written about Liam? I was pining after him for years!' Trinity put her hand to her mouth. Busted. Did that mean she still had feelings for him? Then again, it would explain a lot.

'This is a break-up song, though. It's literally called *The Sinner*. It's three and a half minutes of you playing the martyr because Liam left you for me.'

'And it's—'

'Nothing personal. Yeah, yeah. Broken record.' Fayth ran her hands over her face. They were making zero progress.

Time to change tack. 'How did you feel when you heard about our stalker?'

'I mean, I was horrified that one of my fans could do that. It was such a PR nightmare.'

'There! There it is!' said Fayth, pointing as she spoke. 'No thought for how Liam and I were. No mention of how I ended up in hospital with a concussion, or that our stalker got shot. Just that you were horrified someone associated with you could do what she did, and that it was a PR nightmare.'

'It *was* a PR nightmare, and I *was* horrified one of my fans did it. I always encourage them to be nice to one another, like Ellen!' said Trinity, her voice going up an octave as she spoke.

'Yeah, except Ellen doesn't just say that she's nice – she shows people how to be nice to one another. When was the last time you did something nice for someone?'

'I tried with Hollie and Astin! I was going to have it like a group therapy session. I had it all planned out! They were supposed to be sat next to each other but someone moved the name cards before I got there.'

'You mean like you moved Astin and Jack's onto our table?'

'The HATT kids are so boring,' said Trinity, referring to the boy band they should've been sat with at the charity gala. 'You didn't miss anything.'

'I wouldn't know. I never got the chance to speak to them.'

'Then you'll just have to take my word for it.'

'You mean like I should every time you say that you're just trying to help people?'

'I am! Why don't you believe me?'

'Because,' said Fayth, pulling on her coat, 'no matter what I say or do, you'll always focus on how everything affects you. You don't care about other people's feelings and you never have. I'm done trying to make sense of you. I'm done arguing with you. Do what you want. I don't care any more.'

Three

Fayth slept better that night than she had for a while. Dr Kaur had been right – facing one of the people responsible for her problems had made her feel better. She woke up the next morning in bed alone, the smell of breakfast wafting in from the kitchen. Fayth sat up and stretched. She had Liam. That was all that mattered.

The bedroom door opened. The smell of eggs, fried bread, and cinnamon grew in strength. Liam walked in, carrying a tray with French toast and tea. When they met at the start of the year, he couldn't even make normal toast. Where had he learned to make French toast? She couldn't even make French toast! Not that she couldn't have figured it out if she'd wanted to.

'Morning,' he said as Fayth crossed her legs under the duvet.

'When did you learn to make French toast?' she asked, inhaling the sweet smell of cinnamon and fried bread.

He opened the legs on the tray and placed it over her lap. 'Ola gave me the recipe. I burned the first piece, but it tasted all right. I saved the nice one for you.'

'Thanks,' she said, kissing his cheek. 'But why are you making me breakfast in bed?'

He sat beside her, his legs underneath him. 'What, I can't make you breakfast because I love you?'

Fayth pursed her lips. She didn't want to come across as paranoid. Was breakfast in bed what normal couples did? Patrick had never brought her breakfast in bed. And Liam's lifestyle was hardly normal…

Liam sighed. He ran his hand through his hair. Yep. Something was up. 'Whatever you said to Trinity yesterday…'

'Yes…?' Fayth probed. She'd told him everything when she'd got back. Or at least she'd thought she had. Had she missed something?

'She's written a blog post admitting the song is about us.'

'Ugh.' Fayth closed her eyes. Trinity really never would change. How had Liam put up with her for so long? But then, by trying to be there for her, was he not the better person, given how she treated all her friends? Fayth sighed, opening her eyes. 'You know what? I don't care. Let her say what she wants. She'll never change, and it's pointless to waste so much energy on her.'

Liam tucked her hair behind her ear and kissed her forehead. 'You sure you're all right?'

'Surprisingly,' she said. 'Maybe this therapy malarkey is paying off after all.'

*

'So you don't feel your meeting with Trinity was productive?' said Dr Kaur.

'Not really,' said Fayth with a sigh. She rested her elbows on her lap, and her head in her hands. 'No matter what I say or do, that woman will always hate me. I'll never understand her.'

'What changed your mind about meeting with her? You said last time we spoke that you didn't want to.'

'I guess you made me realise I needed to face my demons and not run away from them. Confronting her seemed like a good way to get closure.'

'That's a very mature way of looking at things.'

'It's a shame the person I met with isn't so mature.'

'Some people never fully grow up,' said Dr Kaur. 'Some

people never learn to control their emotions – they let their emotions control them.'

'She'd probably claim it's good for her creativity.'

'But surely harnessing those emotions and learning to control them would make her more creative, because she could summon them on command?' suggested Dr Kaur.

Fayth shrugged. 'Logic isn't really her thing.'

'From what you've told me over our last few sessions, you've changed a lot since you lost your mother and sister. For you, that was your trigger.'

'My trigger?'

'For everything to change. Some people call it their rock bottom moment. Many of the most successful people in the world have them.'

'They do?'

'Yes. Steve Jobs got fired from Apple – the company he created – then went on to turn Pixar into a multi-billion dollar company. He then returned to Apple and turned its fortune around, too. J. K. Rowling was on benefits before *Harry Potter* was published. Sometimes you have to lose everything to realise what's really important in life.'

'But it was such a long time after losing Mum and Mhairi that things started to change.'

'But you said it yourself – that was what caused you to see your husband differently, and to eventually leave him. And now look at you. Your life may not be perfect, but no one's is. You do have very supportive friends and family, though. And a boyfriend that loves you. What does Trinity have?'

Fayth stared at Dr Kaur. How had she not seen it before? Had someone suggested it and she'd refused to believe it? Probably. But everything finally made sense. 'She's jealous.'

Dr Kaur nodded. 'It's very possible. She may have money, but she clearly craves something more meaningful. And you already have that. You have everything she'll never be able to have: a family, friends, and a partner.'

'But she could easily have those things. That's what I don't get.'

'Could she? Or has she spent so long on her own that she doesn't know how to have real, honest relationships?'

'I never thought of that,' said Fayth.

'We often feel arrogant admitting that someone might be jealous of us, but there's no shame in it. Most bullying stems from some form of great pain. We then take it out on someone we deem weaker than us – or someone who has something that we don't – in order to make ourselves feel better. It isn't healthy, but it's human.'

DECEMBER

One

Fayth's stomach was in knots. It was the day of the photography show and she had no idea what to expect. Would anyone show up? Would anyone like her photos? Would they like them enough to buy them? She'd told Hollie not to travel all the way to New York as it wasn't a big deal, but as she pushed the doors to the gallery open with her sweaty palms, she started to realise it really was a big deal.

If things went well, she could sell her first photograph or even get a job offer. No pressure.

She stepped farther into the room, her camera banging against her stomach. She grabbed hold of it to steady it. Her stomach felt bad enough already.

There was no one else there yet, so the room felt empty and almost creepy with its white walls and photographs all around. Wandering around the room, she studied the photos. They were big. *Really* big. She hadn't expected that. But that made the love and passion that had gone into them even clearer. The stories behind every photo were displayed beside them, along with the prices for different-sized prints. Fayth gravitated to her photo of Liam, which hung opposite the entrance. She was both proud and a little annoyed – were they doing that because they knew it would get people's attention? She'd joked about how Liam's head couldn't get any bigger, but it turned out it could…

It still amazed her that she'd taken that photo. She removed her camera from around her neck and placed it on a table behind her, then stepped closer to the photo. His expression haunted her. He was so much more than the pretty boy he'd been labelled as. Sure, he had pretty eyes and couldn't grow a beard even if he wanted to, but there was a haunted look in his eyes that only came from true pain. He was no naive little boy.

She liked to think that only she could've got a shot of him looking so vulnerable, but since it was his job to play pretend, he could've faked it. But she knew it was real. She knew that he'd let her see him that vulnerable. It was the same look he'd had after their stalker, Tawny, had tried to kill them at the pub. It was a look of guilt: he still blamed himself for having put her in danger.

Something smashed to the floor.

Fayth turned to find her camera on the floor, a huge dent in its side and the lens broken off. The camera had been a present from her dad, her younger sister, and Liam. And judging from the giant dent in it, she wasn't sure it was repairable.

Rupert was walking away, his hands in his pockets. He looked so casual she almost threw the broken camera at the back of his head.

'Hey!' said Fayth, standing up with her crumpled camera in-hand.

Rupert turned around. 'I'm sure your boyfriend can afford to fix it.'

'What?' said Fayth. 'Is that why you've been such a dick to me? Because you don't like who my boyfriend is?'

'I've seen you with your celebrity friends online. You've never worked a day in your life, have you?'

Fayth blinked a few times, trying to process what he'd just said. 'Are you shitting me? Do you seriously think I don't know what it's like to work, or to feel real pain? You have no idea what it cost me to get here. I spent my whole life working in my family's pub. I hadn't even left the UK until a year ago. And you know where that got me? My mum and sister died in a car accident. My husband cheated on me. Someone stalked Liam and me for months and almost killed us. I've been through more than you and your narrow mind could ever possibly imagine.'

Rupert tried to interrupt her, but she ignored him. She hadn't seen or heard anyone else come in. She had no idea if anyone was listening. She didn't care. He'd been a jerk to her for the last three months, and she'd had enough of it.

'How dare you think that you're better than me because you don't have money or famous friends? I haven't used any of Liam's money or influence to get here. You know what money I used? My fucking inheritance. And every time I look at my photos I don't see the subjects of them, I see my mum and sister's faces as their car slid off the road and down a hill. I think about how it should've been me in that car, not them, but I asked to stay at the pub so that I could have some alone time after arguing with my then-husband. So don't you ever tell me that my life is easy, or that I don't know about hard work or pain. You don't fucking know me, and you have no right to judge me you narrow-minded, narcissistic, pretentious arsehole. I hope your narrow-mindedness doesn't rub off on your daughter.' Fayth turned on her heels and stomped off before he could respond. Her hands were curled into fists, her jaw so tight she could hear her teeth grinding together. She stormed out of the gallery and into the cold December air.

And then she began to cry.

Everything she'd said to him was true. She did see her mum and sister's faces every time she looked at her photos. Every time she *took* a photo. Their deaths were what had led to her meeting Liam, and affording her camera, and the photography course, and everything that had happened and would happen since. How was she supposed to deal with that? Would she trade it all in if it meant she could get them back? Not that it mattered. It didn't work like that. They were never coming back.

Arms snaked around her waist, pulling her into the body that they belonged to. She caught a whiff of cinnamon and sandalwood. Liam. She curled into him, sobbing into his Tommy Hilfiger shirt – something that seemed to be one of her favourite hobbies when in New York. She was done with other people's shit. She just needed to cry, dammit, and she knew Liam wouldn't mind. That was why she loved him.

'Sorry I was late,' he said. 'Bloody audition ran over.'

Fayth stifled a laugh. It always sounded funny when Liam used British swear words, but after what had just happened it wasn't nearly as funny as usual. 'Did you hear my, uh, rant?' Fayth asked as her crying began to slow.

'Most of it,' said Liam. 'He had it coming.'

'Mmm,' said Fayth. He was right, but that didn't stop the guilt that was building inside of her. Had she been too harsh? What names, exactly, had she called him? Oh god. Saying all of that didn't make her any better than he was. And she'd thought she'd stopped being easily wound up after letting go of her problems with Trinity.

The gallery door opened, and someone stepped outside. Fayth lifted her head from Liam's shirt to see who it was. She instantly regretted it. It was Rupert.

'Have you got a minute?' he said.

'Sure,' said Fayth, straightening up but not letting go of Liam. His problem was as much with Liam as it was with her. He could say it in front of them both.

'All right then,' said Rupert with a sigh. 'You were right. I shouldn't have judged you based on your boyfriend.'

'No, you shouldn't have,' agreed Fayth. Liam rubbed her arm.

'You're not the typical Hollywood type,' Rupert added.

'I'm not *any* Hollywood type,' she corrected. 'I'm an unemployed bartender from rural Scotland.'

'You don't look like one,' said Rupert.

Liam sniggered.

'What does one look like?' asked Fayth.

'Er...'

'Exactly. Perhaps you should stop judging people based on titles and tabloids and judge them based on morals instead,' said Fayth. She crossed her arms. Liam rubbed her back. For a guy who had an opinion on everything, he was always silent when she confronted someone. Why was that?

'My apology was terrible, wasn't it?' said Rupert.

'Yes.'

Rupert closed his eyes and took a deep breath. 'I'm sorry. You were right. I am pretentious, and I judge people too quickly. I lost my wife last year to cancer. My daughter and I are still healing. I have to protect her. But I don't want to raise her to be judgemental or narrow-minded. That's a ticket to cynicism and unhappiness. She doesn't deserve that. And you didn't deserve for me to break your camera. I'll pay to have it fixed.'

'Money isn't the issue,' said Fayth. 'Not to me, anyway. Is your daughter here now?'

'She's inside.'

Fayth glanced at Liam. He nodded.

*

Rupert's daughter, Olivia, was inside looking at his photos with his mum. They turned around when Fayth, Liam, and Rupert walked in. Olivia beamed. Then her face hardened. She must've remembered their argument about Liam in class a few weeks earlier. It had created such an awkward atmosphere that it had been hard for Fayth to forget, too.

'It's OK, Liv,' said Rupert as they reached his daughter and mum. 'You can talk to him.'

Olivia's face brightened. 'Really?'

He nodded.

Olivia immediately ditched her dad and approached Liam. She held out her hand. 'Hi. I'm Olivia, but you can call me Liv.'

'Hey Liv,' said Liam, shaking her hand.

'How old were you when you made *Rescue Rover*?'

Fayth snorted. It didn't matter how old Liam got, he'd never escape his first film role.

'Ten,' said Liam, appearing unfazed. 'How old are you?'

'Six. Do you think I could be an actor?'

How was he supposed to answer that? That was a trap if she'd ever seen one. Different parents had different views. How could he possibly know how Rupert felt? Some parents were encouraging, others preferred their kids to focus on school. Liam preferred kids to stay out of Hollywood, knowing what life had been like for Tate and Trinity. He'd got off pretty lightly in comparison.

'I think you can be anything you want to be,' said Liam. Fayth had a feeling that was one of his heavily rehearsed stock responses from his PR team. Even so, it was a good one. When you get asked the same question often enough, it's no surprise you go into autopilot sometimes. 'The most important thing is that you work hard and be kind to the people around you.'

Olivia nodded. 'I will, I promise.' She hugged him. He hugged her back.

'Thank you,' said Rupert.

Two

Talking to Rupert made Fayth realise that he wasn't as confident as he pretended to be: he was a scared boy in the body of a man. Much like Trinity was just a scared girl in the body of a woman. The only difference was that Rupert had acknowledged his mistake and apologised. Trinity never would.

Oh, Trinity. All roads in Fayth's mind still led back to her, her stalker Tawny, her mum, or her sister, but she was calmer than she had been in a long time. Talking to Dr Kaur so candidly made her feel like someone truly knew what she was going through. They planned to continue the sessions over Skype when Fayth left New York. It wouldn't be the same, not speaking in-person, but it was better than nothing.

The room filled while Fayth and Rupert talked. Fayth hadn't expected so many people to want to check out an amateur photography exhibition. What if nobody liked the photos? What if nobody bought anything? But then, she knew the photo of Liam was good. She didn't need anyone to tell her that. But really, it was the subject that had made it so good. Not to mention she had several other photos on display. She didn't want the one of Liam to be the main focus, although she knew that it would be.

She found her way to the photo and admired it from the back of the crowd. Maisie came up behind her and beamed. 'Guess who just sold her first photo!'

'You?' said Fayth.

'No, you!' said Maisie.

'That one?' said Fayth, pointing to the photo of Liam.

'Nope,' grinned Maisie.

'No?' said Fayth, her eyes widening.

Maisie jerked her head to the photo on their left. The one of Liesel and Arthur that she'd taken in Central Park. 'That one.'

Fayth smiled. It was such an odd feeling. Someone – she didn't know who, but she was desperate to find out – had spent their money on something she'd created. Something that had only taken her a few seconds to put together, but that had taken years of hard work to be able to create. What would they do with it? Would they hang it on their wall? Put it on the bookshelf? Use it as cat litter? 'Who bought it?'

'Dunno. The gallery doesn't pass on customer information. But does it matter? You just sold you first photo!'

'Yeah,' said Fayth, her cheeks burning.

'Go you!' said Maisie. 'We've only been here an hour and you sold something! At your first exhibition!'

'It's not even a proper exhibition,' mumbled Fayth, staring at the marble floor.

'Would you stop talking yourself down? You did it! Isn't that something to be proud of?'

'Yes it is,' agreed Liam. He kissed her cheek, then turned to his photograph. 'We'll get you out of your self-deprecation yet.'

'That we will,' agreed Maisie.

*

Fayth wasn't used to networking, but she found that it came naturally to her from all her time at the pub. She still hadn't found out who'd bought her photo of Liesel and Arthur, but did it really matter? She wanted to thank them, but then, was that weird? She spotted a figure admiring the photo and wondered if that was the guy that had bought it. Then she realised that it wasn't just any old figure: it was Astin.

'This one's my favourite. You captured their vulnerability and their strength,' said Astin as she came to stand beside him. He adjusted his crutches, half leaning on them, half supporting himself.

'Thanks,' said Fayth. 'It's my favourite too. The couple in the photo are around here somewhere.'

Astin gave a small smile. He stared up at the photo again and sighed. Was he thinking about Hollie? About how he could've had that with her, but he'd thrown it away? There was a longing in his expression. His gaze darted around the room as if he were looking for someone.

Fayth took an educated guess. 'She's not here.'

His body relaxed, but his face fell. 'Oh.'

'You were hoping she would be?'

He shrugged.

'I told her not to bother; it's not that big of a deal.'

'Sure it is,' said Astin. 'You really suck at giving yourself any credit, don't you?'

Fayth gave a small laugh. She'd heard that a lot, lately. Was she really that bad?

Liesel and Arthur walked past, laughing. Astin noticed them and sighed.

'You really suck at giving yourself a break,' said Fayth.

Astin lowered his head and turned away from her. She'd gone too far. That was a horrible thing for her to have said. 'I'm sorry. That was uncalled for.'

'Doesn't make it any less true.'

'You made a mistake,' said Fayth. 'That's allowed.'

'It was more than that. It was…' He shook his head. 'Never mind. This is meant to be about you!'

'I'm here if you want to talk, you know.'

'Thanks, but it's kind of awkward, don't you think?'

'Yeah, I guess so,' admitted Fayth. She *would* feel weird if Astin talked to her about how he was feeling. How would she react if he admitted to her that he was still in love with Hollie? Not that it wasn't written all over his face anyway, but if he admitted it to her, would she have to tell Hollie? Would Hollie even want to know?

He touched the spot between his shoulder blades where he'd had the surgery. 'I still feel it sometimes, where my back hit the camera crane. I don't remember much, but I have flashbacks.'

'Me too,' said Fayth, touching the back of her head where the gun had hit her skull. She'd been lucky it hadn't done any long-term damage. 'None of it was your fault, you know that, right?'

'Sure it was,' said Astin, tapping one of his crutches against the lino. 'I could've talked to someone about my concerns with Roskowski's direction. I could've been nicer to Hollie. I could've been nicer to everyone.' He sighed. 'Learn from your mistakes, right?'

'Right,' said Fayth. He looked so broken. She wished there was something she could do to help, but she knew all too well Astin was too prideful to ever accept any help.

'I should get going,' said Astin. 'Congrats again.'

'Thanks,' said Fayth. She didn't know what else to say. Was it even her place to say anything? 'It was good to see you,' was all she managed to say as he turned and walked away.

*

By the end of the night, almost all of the photos had sold. Most of the ones that remained belonged to Rupert. Fayth studied his photos to try to work out what was missing. It was pretty obvious that he hadn't learned as much everyone else. The angles weren't quite right; the depth of focus that he'd attempted in one was too much, making the photo too blurry. His narrow-mindedness had its consequences.

'Karma sucks,' said Rupert, joining her beside a photo

of his dog.

'I don't believe in karma,' said Fayth.

'You don't?'

'No. I believe we get what we put into life. The harder you work, the greater the rewards.'

'So you're saying I didn't work hard enough?'

She turned to him. 'Did you? Or did you think you already knew everything?'

Rupert stared at his shoes. 'I wanted to do the course, but every time Jasper told me to do something differently to what I was used to, I ignored him. I didn't like being told what to do.'

'And now?'

'Now I'm going to learn from my mistakes, look back on my notes, and work on my photography. There might be some gaps in my notes from where I ignored him, though.'

'I can email you mine if you like,' said Fayth.

'I'd appreciate that.'

*

In just a couple of days, Fayth would be back home in Scotland. Except it didn't feel like home any more. Not after everything that had happened not just there, but in New York, too. She leaned her head against the Jag's headrest as Thalia drove them back to the apartment. It had been a fun night – one she hadn't wanted to end – but she knew all too well she couldn't stop time from moving forwards.

'Excited for the holidays?' asked Liam.

'I guess,' said Fayth. 'It will be weird being back in Scotland again.' Ever since she'd lost her mum and sister, she'd hated Christmas. It just wasn't the same. Liam knew her pain – he'd lost his older sister, too – but he and his family always went on holiday to some exotic location. He'd invited her, but she couldn't leave her dad and sister. Not when it was their first Christmas without the pub.

Being back in Scotland would also mean being without Liam again. She'd got used to having him around, and she wasn't ready to give that up. They hadn't come up with any plans to meet up again though, which meant the long-distance thing. Ugh.

'So where to after that?' said Liam, draping his arm across the back of the seats. Fayth leaned into him.

'What do you mean?'

'Where's our next adventure?'

'You haven't got bored of me yet, then?'

'Not yet, although we might be getting close. It's a good job you're going to see your family over the holidays.'

'Yeah, you're starting to annoy me a bit too,' she joked.

'Does that mean I can't join you and Hollie in Barcelona?'

Fayth's heart leapt. 'You're coming to Barcelona?'

'Well I was planning to, but if you're bored of me…'

'No! I'm not bored of you. There's plenty of room in the apartment Tate found. I'm sure she and Hollie won't mind.'

'Wait. The three of you are renting an apartment together?'

'Yeah,' said Fayth. 'Think you can manage in an apartment with the three of us?'

Liam hesitated for a moment. 'Jury's still out.'

Three

When Astin returned home, he found his apartment door already unlocked. What the hell? He opened the door with one hand, his other curled tightly around his crutches. Should he call out, see who was there?

'SURPRISE!' shouted Jack, appearing from the living room.

Astin jumped. 'Dude, what the hell?'

'Good to see you too,' said Jack. He hugged his roommate.

'I thought you were in Bali on a yoga retreat?'

Jack shrugged. 'Got bored. Missed New York. And my favourite roomie.'

'Sure you did,' said Astin. His heart was thudding in his chest. It was just Jack. He was harmless. Mostly. Definitely more harmless since he'd been sober.

'So, what'd I miss?' Jack asked as they made their way into the living room.

'Not much,' said Astin. He dumped his crutches by the side of the sofa, then sat down. Taking his phone from his pocket, he flicked through his emails. Jack rambled on about something, but Astin lost track of what it was when he saw an email from one of the producers of *Knight of Shadows*.

'What's with the face?' asked Jack, jumping over the back of the sofa and sitting beside him.

'One of the producers of *Knight of Shadows* just sent me the premier dates.'

'Well you did work on the film. Why wouldn't they invite

you?'

'I was nearly killed on that set!'

'So maybe going would get you some closure.'

'Are you for real? I can't do that.'

'Why not?'

'Roskowski will be there! He's the reason I ended up in a wheelchair and can never do stunt work again!'

'You're suing the guy. You'll have to see him again eventually anyway. And for all you know, you could be able to do stunt work again. Nobody has checked you over lately, have they? Since when were you one to listen to other people's advice anyway?'

Astin glared at him.

'What? It's true.'

Astin continued to glare. 'I can't go. I just can't.'

Jack scoffed. 'Because you're doing a real good job of dealing with things right now.'

Would it really be good for him to go to the premier of the film that had almost killed him? Would his failed stunt end up in the final cut? Had they rewritten that scene or used someone else after he'd been injured? Had they CGIed it? He could go and find out, or he could just ask someone who'd worked on it and save himself the trouble.

But maybe Jack was right.

Maybe he did need closure.

Was that what his problem was? Was that what had pulled him back to New York, or was it just that where he'd grown up no longer felt like home?

He flicked through the premier dates and locations again. LA. London. Hong Kong. Barcelona.

What Happens in Barcelona preview

Trinity almost choked on the gin she was drinking. 'Jealous? Don't flatter yourself.'

'Then why are you really here? Why did you come all the way to Barcelona?'

'I told you – I was at an event! It's not my fault they didn't invite you because you're a fucking flake.'

'*I'm* the flake? That's rich!'

'Right, because I'm the one that used to turn up late to set,' said Trinity, rolling her eyes.

'I was grieving!'

'And getting high.'

'You don't get to judge me,' said Liam, crossing his arms.

'What, but you get to judge me? You get to tell me the best way to deal with this shit life that I've been given? You get to control me, like everyone else?'

'I'm not trying to control you! Why can't you see that!'

Trinity took the gin bottle, opened the terrace doors, and stepped outside. Cold air swept through the suite. It was a clear but windy day. It wasn't the kind of day to hang out on the terrace. She turned back to Liam. 'You can leave now.'

He followed her on to the terrace. 'I want to help you. What's so wrong with that?'

'You gave up your chance to help me when you dumped me. You don't get to judge me *and* help me. That's not how you help people. Not unless you want to push them farther into their black hole.' Is that what he'd done by trying to help her?

'If you don't want my help, why do you keep showing up? Why were you at Tate's charity gala? Why did you reach out to Fayth in New York? Why are you *here*?'

'This is *Hollywood*, Liam! It's a small world. It's difficult *not* to run into each other. Not every decision I make is about you.' She climbed on to the edge of the terrace and looked over it. The stone wall was just wide enough to hold her feet.

'Come down from there Trinity, it's dangerous.'

'Oh, stop it, would you? Do you ever take risks? Do you ever do anything outside of your comfort zone?'

'You're standing on the edge of a terrace several stories up. That's not taking a risk. That's playing with fire.'

'Then let the fire rage on.' She took a swig of gin and stumbled. Liam reached out to help her. She regained her balance on her own. 'If I'm the fire, you're the water that's trying to put me out. You're right. We never would've worked together.'

No. That's not right. He wasn't trying to kill her fire. He'd never do that to her. To anyone. Would he? *Had he*?

'I didn't do that. I wouldn't do that,' he said, half trying to convince himself.

'Whatever,' said Trinity. 'You can go back to your apple-pie life now.'

'It's not an apple-pie life! Does she make me happy? Yes. Are we perfect? No. But no couple is.'

Trinity laughed. It was shrill, high-pitched; almost like a cackle. He'd never heard her make that noise before, not even when playing the villain in *Highwater*. 'So, what? You can accept her faults but not mine? You can give her a second chance when she makes a mistake, but you couldn't even listen to me when I tried to explain to you why I was back on the coke? Let's face it, Liam: you never really cared. You wanted to care, but really, you liked the attention that I gave you. I was something stable for you to cling to after rehab. I wouldn't suffocate you like your parents would've if you'd stayed with them, or like your staff wanted to. I let you be you, but you could never let me be me.'

'That's not true! Stop saying that!'

'Oh, Liam. You really have never been any good at seeing what's right in front of you.'

'What's that supposed to mean?'

Trinity stared at the gin bottle. There were only a few drops left in it. She tilted her head back, pouring the liquid down her throat. Then she fell.

What happens next? Find out in What Happens in Barcelona, *out now in ebook and print!*

Hollywood Gossip preview

I cleared my throat. I'd come back from lunch to find Jack asleep under a table in the control room. He'd pulled his orange floral bomber jacket over his head, no doubt to block out the bright lights.

When I walked in, he looked up at me sheepishly through his deep brown eyes. His afro had been squashed by the floor he'd fallen asleep on, but it looked like it had seen better days anyway. It was in need of some serious moisturiser. Those split ends needed to be cut, too.

While I admired his devil-may-care attitude, so far I wasn't impressed with his work ethic. We had a song to record and only two days to do it. If he wasn't going to help me, or he was going to slow things down, I'd have to find someone else.

'I…uh…hi,' he said. He tried to sit up but hit his head on the table instead. Idiot. 'Who put that there?'

'Who put *you* there?' I said, scowling. I'd been gone less than half an hour and he'd fallen asleep? And not even in a chair, but under a table! Lazy much?

He crawled out from under the table then sat on one of the swivel chairs beside the controls. Instead of looking like he was actually interested in working together, he rested his elbows on the desk and his head in his hands. He smelled like a bottomless vat of vodka. It was disgusting.

'Excuse you?' I said.

'Hmm?' he said, tilting his head toward me.

'We have a song to write,' I reminded him.

'Oh. Yeah.' He turned his head back so that his palms were pressing into his eyes.

I crossed my arms over my chest and tapped my foot.

He turned and glared at me. 'Do you mind? That's really annoying.'

Wow.

'He-*llo*? Have you forgotten why we're here? Are you even going to *try* to get some work done today?'

How do they go from this to one of Hollywood's greatest power couples? Find out in Hollywood Gossip, *out now in ebook and print! The course of true love never did run smooth, and that's never been more true than for Tate and Jack.*

Behind the Spotlight preview

I was in the stockroom, unpacking a bunch of Adele CDs, when they walked in. The joker. The quiet one. The dancer. And him.

Oh, and their entourage. No boy band is complete without their entourage.

I hadn't seen him in almost five years. I looked the same, maybe a little chubbier. Luke was almost unrecognisable from the guy I'd gone to sixth form with. His mousy hair was bleached and styled into a quiff that defied the laws of physics. He didn't wear graphic tees from H&M any more, either: it looked like all his clothes cost more than I'd earn in a day. Maybe a week.

The grungy fashion reject I'd once known was gone. The baggy t-shirts he used to favour were now tight-fitting, hinting at the muscle underneath. His choice on that day – or, more than likely, someone else's – was a pair of cigarette jeans and a blue and white stripy t-shirt. He looked like a Paul Smith model.

Their entourage – which seemed to consist mostly of burly security guards – tailed them, all speaking into phones and headsets and looking more organised and put-together than I felt.

I ducked behind a shelving unit, wishing I were invisible. It's not easy to hide when you're well over six feet tall.

He had no idea I worked there, but that didn't mean he wouldn't recognise me.

None of my coworkers knew about our history together

though.
I wanted to keep it that way.

Find out what happens next in Behind the Spotlight, out now in ebook and print!

Discover Liam's Story

Puppy-dog eyes. Prince Charming. Hollywood heartthrob. Liam York has a lot of nicknames. None of them mention the demons that chase him every day.

He may be worth millions, but underneath it all? He's human, just like us. And if he doesn't do something soon, those demons are going to catch up to him.

Intrigued? Get your copy of *The Real World*, available exclusively to mailing list subscribers from my website: www.kristinaadamsauthor.com/the-real-world

Also by Kristina Adams

What Happens in Hollywood Universe

What Happens in…
    The Real World
    What Happens in New York
    What Happens in London
    Return to New York
    What Happens in Barcelona
    What Happens in Paphos

Hollywood Gossip
    Hollywood Gossip
    Hollywood Parents
    Hollywood Drama
    Hollywood Destiny
    Hollywood Heartbreak
    Hollywood Romance

Standalones
    Behind the Spotlight
    Hollywood Nightmare

Boxsets
- Welcome to the Spotlight
- What Happens in… books 1 and 2
- What Happens in… books 3 - 5
- What Happens in… the Complete Collection
- Hollywood Gossip books 1 - 3

Nonfiction
- How to Write Believable Characters
- Writing Myths
- Productivity for Writers

Poetry
- Revenge of the Redhead

Writing as K.C. Adams

Afterlife Calls
- The Ghost Hunter's Haunting
- The Ghost's Call
- The Mummy's Curse
- The Necromancer's Secret
- The Witch's Sacrifice
- The Mean Girl's Murder
- The Poltergeist's Ship
- The Dead Man's Blood

About the Author

Kristina Adams is the author of 19 novels, 3 books for writers, and too many blog posts to count. She publishes mother/daughter ghost stories as K.C.Adams. When she's not writing, she's playing with her dog or inflicting cooking experiments on her boyfriend. If you're wondering about the greenhouse mentioned in her previous bio, it didn't survive.

Printed in Great Britain
by Amazon